THE LIBRARY

THE LIBRARY

WHERE LIFE CHECKS OUT

CARMEN DESOUSA

The Library

(Where Life Checks Out)

Copyright© 2014 by Carmen DeSousa

ISBN: 9781945143182

www.CarmenDeSousaBooks.com

Cover Design by Melinda De Ross

Library Interior Image Credit: Anyaivanova

Woman on Cover Image Credit: CaptBlack76

This is a fictional work. All characters and events in this publication, other than those clearly in the public domain, are solely the concepts and products of the author's imagination or are used to create a fictitious story and should not be construed as real. Any resemblance to real persons, living or dead, is purely coincidental.

All rights reserved. No part of this book may be used or reproduced, stored in a retrieval system, or transmitted, in any form by any means, without the prior permission in writing, except in the case of brief quotations, reviews, and articles.

For any other permission, book club visits, signings, or library copies, please visit the about section at www.carmendesousabooks.com.

About This Book

Dear Reader,

I originally wrote *The Depot (When Life and Death Cross Tracks)* as a follow-up novelette to *The Pit Stop (This Stop Could be Life or Death)*, but my wonderful readers asked for more. So since I always listen to my readers, here you are! Part one is the original thirteen-thousand-word novelette, *The Depot (When Life and Death Cross Tracks)*. Part two is the follow-up novel, *The Library (Where Life Checks Out)*.

Happy Reading!

Carmen

A Ghost Story

In 1989, I worked at a restaurant in Rockledge, Florida called Ashley's Cafe. Although fictional, my idea for *The Depot* and *The Library* stemmed from the ghost who haunts the 1930s tavern.

My fascination with the restaurant came about the first night I served as the restaurant's general manager. I'd worked there for almost two years and had never heard or saw a thing, but my first night in my new position was a different story. It's been so long, I barely remember all that happened, but one thing that I'll never forget is one of those large oval trays — that can't possibly balance on its side — came sliding across the floor at me. Also, a five-gallon bucket of water spilled across the floor when no one was near it. Maybe the ghost was just reminding me who was boss.

A Ghost Story

But the most nerve-wracking occurrences throughout the years were the number of employees — including myself — who felt as though someone had pushed them down the service stairs.

My husband — who happened to be a police officer at the time — also got to hear all the stories from the other officers who'd searched the café in the middle of the night because of alarm calls. Unfortunately, he doesn't have any stories, but the detective's account in The Depot is based off several officers whom my husband knew and trusted.

Since I'd always been interested in the supernatural, I researched the death of the woman who supposedly haunts Ashley's via microfilm from the old library in Cocoa, Florida.

At the time, her death was on record as one of the most heinous murders in Florida's history. The murderer went through great lengths to conceal the woman's identity, including smashing out all her teeth, cutting off her fingers, and burning her body. According to witnesses, the woman had been dating someone from power and wealth. And to my surprise, when I looked forward past a few days, the story had all but disappeared. Weeks later, nothing! Think about that! One of the most shocking crimes in Florida's history in the thirties, and the newspaper drops the story.

Yeah ... things that make you say, "Hmmm ..."

So, there you have it. While my story is fictional, there is a ghost story. Maybe the ghost of Ethel Allen will haunt that restaurant until someone uncovers the truth about her murder.

For you ghost hunters who'd like to read more about Ashley's ghost, click here.

Part One

The Depot
(When Life and Death Cross Tracks)

PROLOGUE

Edda should have known he'd deny her. Deny seeing her, deny being with her. Her friend had warned her, but she'd thought he was her chance to escape the life she'd been living. A chance to be someone. A chance at love.

Ever since she'd moved out of her momma's home, life had been difficult. She could barely even pay her way at the boarding house where she stayed. At nineteen, the only thing she had going for her was her looks and body, even though it'd been a challenge getting her size back down to fit the few clothes she owned.

Wesley had assured her that he'd take care of her. But seeing his face tonight, she knew it had all been lies. He screamed that everything was her fault and that he couldn't be bothered with someone of her social status. He'd continued to shout while she shielded her ears, attempting to drown out his obscenities and threats of what he planned to do to her.

She opened the door of the bar, hoping her best friend was still working and could give her a ride home. As soon as she stepped onto the polished wood floors, she noticed the mess she was making. Black mud covered her new patent leather shoes. Then she saw her new dress she'd ordered from the Sears, Roebuck, and Co. Catalog. It had taken months to save $9.98, and she'd spent it all on one silk crepe satin dress. But she had wanted to look nice when Wesley took her to meet his parents. Now the dress was in shreds.

How had it happened?

Her eyes darted around the bar, trying to remember how she'd gotten back here after her fight with Wesley.

"Becky," she called to her friend, relieved that she was still working. "Throw me a towel, will ya? I got mud all over the new floors."

Her friend ignored her, as did everyone else crowded around the bar. The patrons laughed and sang along with the piano man in the corner, but no one had turned to look at her, even when the bells over the door had announced her arrival.

"Becky," she said louder. Still, no one acknowledged her.

Instead, bodies of people rushed around her, their faces contorting and blurring as though she were in a dream or whooshing by them in an automobile. Men with mustaches and beards reshaped to smooth-skinned faces belonging to women, then back to men again. Pale-white faces turned dark, then back to white, and then every shade in between. The clothes they wore changed colors, fabrics, even styles. Dresses went from short to longer lengths and then to short again. Business suits and ties changed to dungarees and undershirts. The room lightened and darkened, over and over, as though the sun were circling the tavern within seconds. The thick-waxed floor below her dulled and then disappeared, and within seconds, a new floor had taken its place. Tables spun before her, along with the chairs, as if some invisible entity were installing them and removing them repeatedly, as though they couldn't make up their mind what style of furniture they wanted.

Her gaze dropped to her hands, noticing thick black

blood dripped from her fingertips. The droplets fell, but never landed.

She searched the room, hoping someone would help her, but the entire room flashed in front of her, similar to when Becky and she'd gone to the matinee a few months ago and seen *The Thin Man*. When the movie was over, they'd sat and watched as the projector rewound, reversing the entire movie ten times faster than they'd watched it. Only, the scene in the bar seemed to be moving forward, as if the room had sped up.

When the world stopped spinning and twining, Edda raked her eyes across the room, but nothing was the same.

The bar had transformed.

It was the same, but different. A light from the corner of the room drew her attention. It resembled the screen at the show, but smaller. Colorful, bright images of moving pictures flashed on the tiny screen.

Her gaze fell on the two remaining people behind the bar.

Watching them, a fiery hatred singed her insides, causing a flaring passion to radiate through her soul as she realized what had happened to her.

Rather, what he had done to her.

CHAPTER 1

Detective Mark Waters stretched his long legs beneath his favorite corner table of the dimly lit restaurant. Other than alarm calls as a patrol officer, he only came here for lunch, and his table was always open because most customers don't want to sit in the corner where they can't watch TV or view the outside patio area.

From his vantage point, though, he could see the entry, the downstairs seating area, the booths surrounding the bar, the upstairs dining area, and the hanging plants that swung gently overhead. Several minutes had ticked by since the train had passed within thirty feet of the building, and yet, the dangling green vines above the bar swayed, as though dancing to a song only they could hear.

Despite the ghost stories, he loved the old building that dated back to the late 1800s. It had history and character. The famous haunt had been a train station, a brothel, a boarding house, a saloon, and then finally the food and spirits eatery it is today.

He sat within inches of the small restroom where many of the supposed occurrences had taken place. Close enough that if a mouse crawled across the linoleum floor, he'd hear it. He'd had to enter the ancient structure countless times as a patrol officer when the alarm went off at four a.m. It'd happened so many times that the owner had given the police station a key.

A different reason brought him here tonight. Death. Something he'd never escape, since he'd decided to follow in his father's footsteps as a homicide detective. His father had been dead for almost twenty years, and he was still trying to earn his respect.

"Waters," called the pudgy, seasoned detective from behind the bar. Detective Tim Townsend had always taken it upon himself to throw back a couple of shots when he came here on a midnight call. Townsend had done the same thing on Mark's first call to the restaurant when he was his FTO. When

The Library

Townsend was his field-training officer, Mark wouldn't have dared to utter a word, but now he held rank as lieutenant.

"You better put a five in the till, Townsend. And you better not have more than one."

"Yeah, yeah, I hear ya." Townsend pulled out a bill that Mark was certain was a one and shoved it into the slit of the drawer of the outdated cash register. "But like I was sayin' ..." Townsend squeezed his large belly through the bar entrance and walked over to where Mark sat. He rested his hand on the ladies' bathroom door, but then removed it as if it'd burnt him, and instead, leaned against the solid wood bar. "Did I tell you about the time I was searchin' The Depot and got stuck in that little hall in the ladies' bathroom?"

Mark rested his chin on his fist, resisting the urge to roll his eyes. "Several times."

"Really, Dude. Look." Townsend reached out, opened the ladies' bathroom door, and pointed. "I can't even fit in between those two doors. And yet, I turned and banged on every wall, and I couldn't get out. Larry was here; he heard it."

Mark sighed in response to Townsend's claim, several officers' claims actually. But he'd been coming here for years, and he'd never heard a peep or seen an apparition, as had been claimed for years by officers, customers, and naturally, the owners.

Mark was sure the proprietors loved the extra business they'd received since the TV show *American Haunts* had featured the restaurant. According to the story on the back of the menu, the show had even brought in a medium who had, in fact, sensed several presences.

"I know, I know," Mark said. "The Depot is haunted. I've heard all the stories."

Townsend shook his head and returned to leaning against the bar. "What are we waitin' for?"

"Forensics. What else?"

The hardened detective raised his hands. "Why? Dude jumped in front of a train. End of story. Guess we'll have another lost soul wandering around the old joint." Townsend chuckled at his attempted joke, but then darted his eyes around the eerie edifice as if the dead man might appear because of his callous comment.

Mark huffed out a breath and rubbed his head. "You sound like a teenager for God's sake, not a forty-five-year-old man."

The middle-aged man shrugged as a dismissal. Townsend had never cared what people thought of him, a characteristic Mark admired in the burnt-out detective. "Wife and son moved back." He adjusted his belt around his large waistline. "Guess the punk wears off on me. Kid can't seem to call me anything but *dude*. But hey, at least we're talking."

Mark lifted his chin in acknowledgement. "Congratulations, man. That's great." Considering Townsend probably called his son punk to his face, sort of accounted for the *dude* instead of *dad*. That wouldn't have happened in his house. Even at eight, Mark remembered his father demanding reverence. Of course, his father had doled out respect also. His father had always spoken to him as though he were much older and would frequently discuss the cases he was working, almost as though Mark were his sounding board.

The older detective puffed out his chest a fraction, then scraped a barstool across the floor to sit. "So ... how're things with you, Waters? Any new lady friends you care to share some salacious details on? Since we're just sittin' here."

Mark shook his head. Townsend was the horniest man he knew, probably the reason his wife kept leaving him. If he wasn't picking up a new woman, he was looking for juicy tidbits from the other cops at the department. Mark never shared stories. Not that he had anything interesting to reveal even if he wanted. His sex life had been practically nonexistent for the last couple of years. His job was his lover, and she kept him busy day and night. At twenty-eight, he should be thinking about a wife and kids, but his father had waited until he was forty to marry, so he had time.

"What did you say?" Mark asked the detective who had wandered behind the bar again, sniffing around the booze.

Townsend tilted his head as he held up a bottle of the cheap stuff this time, requesting permission. "I asked if you had any new lady friends."

"I mean after that."

"Nothin', man."

"You didn't mutter something under your breath?"

"You know me, Waters. If I've got somethin' to say, I'll say it."

Mark did know that. Still, he could have sworn he heard him whisper something.

The bells over the door sounded, and the forensic team — all two of them — stepped inside the bar. "You tending bar tonight, Townsend?" Roland bellowed.

"Nah ... just checking stuff."

The Library

Roland laughed. "Sure ya are ... Where's the human hamburger?"

As Mark crossed the room to greet Roland, he gestured toward the rear exit. "It's not pretty."

The head of forensics shook his head. "Never is, Waters. But hell, when you've seen death as many times as I have, you hardly even notice the smell."

"Well, there isn't a death-smell yet. Just that uncooked-meat odor that keeps me from cleaning raw chicken at home."

Roland walked out the rear door, and his new forensic partner Anna — who'd started in the last few months — followed Roland outside, casting a quick glance in Mark's direction.

As good as Anna looked, Mark averted his eyes, trying to ignore his attraction. It was merely the reddish-blond hair, he told himself. He'd always been a sucker for strawberry blondes. But the last time he'd dated a woman close to his job had not worked out well, so he ignored his desire. He was great at ignoring his wants, since he'd been doing it so long.

The door creaked open again. Surprised, Mark turned toward it. He hadn't expected anyone other than the two of them. It closed after lolling open a couple of seconds. He walked to it and pulled it closed until the latch clicked. Anna obviously hadn't realized that old buildings required extra attention, unlike new hardware that closed on its own for energy savings.

"Ready?" Townsend's booming voice rang in his ear at the same time his heavy hand clamped onto Mark's shoulder.

"Yeah." Mark turned, laughing. "You scared the —" He swallowed his words as he noticed Townsend was still behind the bar.

CHAPTER 2

Ashlyn didn't waste any time the following morning. When her alarm sounded at six a.m., she jumped out of bed and scurried to her closet to pull on jeans and a sweatshirt. It wasn't as if she even needed the alarm, since she'd never fallen asleep. How could she possibly have slept after what had happened?

She brushed her teeth in lightning speed. Hesitantly, afraid of what she might see, she examined herself in the mirror. The marks surrounding her neck were already yellow and blue. She ran back to the closet and found an old turtleneck sweater she hadn't worn in years. The weather was still cool enough that no one would question her. They'd just wonder why she was wearing something so unfashionable when she was always the height of fashion.

She'd found out a long time ago that her looks would only take her so far. If she wanted to make it in this world, she had to be someone. At twenty-two, she was close to getting her undergrad degree. 'Course, she couldn't care less to work her way to the top of the corporate ladder; she wanted to run her own company. Her sights were on meeting a successful businessman. After she finished her classes for the day, she used to head to a different coffee shop or hotel bar, always on the lookout. In the evenings, she tended bar because it was the easiest way to make the most amount of money in the least amount of hours. Also, there was always the likely chance she'd meet the man of her dreams as he was leaving work or having a meeting with other wealthy men.

Almost every dime she earned went to her apartment, her car, her appearance, whatever it took to get what she wanted. And she had thought that she had found her golden ticket. Until she had gone and screwed up. She had actually liked Devin, maybe even loved him. Foolish! She had never considered, never expected what he was capable of. She still couldn't believe it.

The Library

Choking back the tears as she thought about everything that had happened wasn't easy, but she had to ignore it and get there. She ran to her Jetta, hopped in, and sped toward the restaurant. She chanced a glimpse at the clock as she raced down the highway: 6:30. Good. She still had a little over an hour before the owners showed.

When Ashlyn arrived, she parked on the far south side of the building, away from employee parking. If anyone drove by, they'd assume she left her car there overnight. It wasn't an unusual occurrence. She always moved her car around before it got dark, so she wouldn't be walking across a pitch-black parking lot by herself at three a.m. As she neared the door, she spotted Devin's Jaguar Convertible and the police tape surrounding it. They must have assumed it was his since it was the only car left in the parking lot. The slanted headlights of the XKR-S seemed to follow her as she raced toward the entry.

Since she was usually the last one to leave, she had her own set of keys. In the beginning, the owner had returned nightly to shut down the business. But after three years of service, Steve trusted her to lock up. She'd never realized how important that was before now. Then again, if he'd been there last night, maybe it wouldn't have happened.

Her hands trembled as she fumbled with the keys in the front door. Her boss would be here by eight, so she had to hurry. She emptied the contents of her drawer into the bank bag and sprinted upstairs to the office where she was supposed to lock up her money after her shift. She struggled with that key too, her heart racing even faster than it had the previous evening. She should have already done this, but she had been so scared and wanted to leave before the police arrived.

Once inside, she grabbed the key out of the desk drawer and dragged a chair to the wall, carefully balancing as she stood so she could reach the overhead cabinet. Steve wasn't technical. If she replaced the tape, he'd never know. Unfortunately, she didn't have time to check what was on it. She'd have to grab it, replace it with the tape from the previous evening, and get out. The system they used was simple; he'd shown it to her once when they had gone on vacation and needed her to help watch the place. All he did was rotate the previous night's tape to the rear and insert the front tape in the machine. He kept thirty days' worth in the event he had to research anything. Truly, the security tapes were to watch employees. But if a robbery ever occurred, the owner would catch it on tape. And since all employees knew this practice, nothing went missing. Steve couldn't afford for bottles of liquor or New York strip steaks to grow legs and walk out the door.

Ashlyn felt horrible betraying her boss' trust, but this had nothing to do with them and everything to do with her. She wasn't sure how much was on that tape, but she knew she would be the first person the police would question in Devin's death.

CHAPTER 3

Mark rolled to a seated position in bed, but sat there rubbing his eyes. He reached for his iPhone, focusing on the bright-white numbers.

Three hours of sleep. Today was going to be rough.

It was doubtful that Townsend had filled out the report to the captain's satisfaction, so more than likely he'd have to do it again.

He stumbled to the coffee maker, but then thought better of it. He needed to get to the station. Instead, he decided on a cold shower, which would not only wake him up, but the negative ions caused by the cold water hitting the tile would also help him think and work through the details of the man's death.

Devin Burke had turned twenty-five last month,

and judging by his driver's license image, he was an attractive man. What made a twenty-five-year old, obviously wealthy man, based on what he drove, commit suicide?

Not that there were ever any answers to that question, but he still wondered. His father's death was thought to be a suicide, and it had turned out to be a murder, so he never presumed the cause of death until he completed his investigation.

Mark had barely sat down behind his desk when Captain Andrew Davis barged into the detective's division, making a beeline toward his cubicle. He'd been right; Townsend must have screwed up the paperwork.

"Waters," the captain shouted. As usual, no pleasantries. "We got an ID on your stiff."

Not sure if it was a statement or a question, Mark nodded, acknowledging that they did have an ID, though tentative until Mark found out if Townsend had reached the next of kin. "Devin Burke, according to his driver's license and the fact that his Jaguar was the only car in the parking lot," Mark offered.

Captain Davis shook his head. "I wasn't asking, Waters. We got an ID. The dead kid's father came down this morning and identified his body, and he's ticked."

"About?"

Captain threw up his hands, pacing in front of Mark's desk. "Who the hell knows? He's wealthy and connected. Wants to know why we don't have the Pennsylvania State Police searching for the murderer."

"*Murderer*, sir?"

"Yeah, yeah, I know. Told the father it was cut-and-dried. Looked like a suicide." Captain Davis plopped down in the chair opposite Mark and leaned forward, resting both elbows on the desk. "Now the commissioner of the State Police is breathing down my neck; evidently he and the kid's father are good friends." Davis blew out a breath that reeked of a cheap cigar. "You ready for this, Waters? Or should I get another detective? You've only been doing this for what ... five years?"

"Seven, sir. Five on the street and two in homicide."

The captain winked. "I knew that, son. Just pullin' your chain. You're exactly like your old man. I have faith in you, but the media's gonna be all over this, looking for someone to lynch. They'll want their fall guy. So if you don't find 'em, they'll accept you instead."

Mark cringed. "Got it."

"They already love you after you solved that twenty-year-old mystery with Gino Canale. I'm sure your father was smiling down on you for avenging his death."

Mark couldn't help but sigh. *Avenging his death?* "Somehow it didn't feel like that, sir, but thank you. I was grateful to know that my father hadn't committed suicide, as the M.E. originally suggested."

Davis stood and held out his hand. "For the record, I never thought that, Waters."

Mark accepted the captain's outreached hand. "Thank you, sir."

"Now, get to work and clear this case quickly." Davis walked toward the door and opened it, but then turned back to him. "But first fix that crap Townsend turned in. We obviously hired him before we required a high school diploma. Was he half-drunk after leaving The Depot or can he not spell?" Davis let the door slam behind him.

Mark turned and eyed Townsend, who was acting as though he were engrossed in the newspaper. Although he probably was. Either the sports page or the comic strips one. Mark entered Townsend's cubicle and slammed the paper down in front of him.

"Where's the report? I swear Townsend ... If I have to keep doing your work, I'm putting you in for a transfer to PEO."

Townsend jumped to his feet. "You wouldn't!"

Mark laughed. "Try me. Nothing like being called a meter maid when you're a *dude*, huh? I'm sure your kid'll get a kick out of that."

"That's plain ornery," Townsend sulked.

"Yeah, well, life sucks and then you die." Mark walked to his desk and scooped up his keys. "Have that report sparkling and on my desk by the time I return, or I'll start filing the papers."

"Where ya going?"

"To The Depot." Mark turned to Townsend, who stood there like a pup wanting to go for a ride. "Didn't you hear? I gotta go solve an unsolvable crime."

CHAPTER 4

Mark followed Steve Baxter upstairs into his office of The Depot. The owner of the establishment held the door open for Mark to enter. The man obviously didn't have a self-esteem issue based on the size of the tiny room. The area was about four-foot deep and at most, eight-foot long. The only things inside the office were a laminate desk, an old metal filing cabinet, and a PVC shelf that held a few stock items with a built-in cupboard above it. Obviously the owner had just pulled a small office together out of hand-me-down office equipment.

"It's up here," Steve said after grabbing a key out of the desk drawer to unlock the miniature doors housing the security tapes. It amazed Mark how lax business owners were with keys. "I installed the cameras a few years ago after cases of meat kept disappearing. I have one on the bar, one on the door, one in the kitchen, and another aimed at the storage shed out back. That's the view you'll be able to see the train tracks. All the cameras are on motion detectors, so as long as *someone* is there, it's filming." The man laughed. "It's never caught our ghost unfortunately." Steve reached to the back of the cabinet, grabbed the cassette, and hopped off the chair he'd scooted in front of the shelving system. "I already changed out the tape before you called this morning. I've gotten in the habit of doing it before I prepare the bank deposit."

Mark listened to the man ramble as he peered out the two-foot square window. According to accounts, the woman who haunted the place had been known to stand at this window. Mark couldn't help but laugh at that one. If she were a ghost, couldn't she materialize through the walls if she wanted to see out?

He turned toward the man and accepted the tape. "I also need a list of whoever worked yesterday."

The owner cocked his head. "I'm confused. I thought you said the man jumped in front of the train?"

Mark shrugged. "My job is to check everything, sir."

His job didn't entail answering *everyone's* questions. And there were always questions. The closer their proximity to the deceased or the scene, the more they thought he owed them answers. Mark never obliged until he had his answers first.

Steve removed a bright blue pushpin holding a computer-printed calendar on a corkboard organizer. He jotted down the names on the paper and handed it to Mark. "Anything else, Detective? Otherwise, I need to get to work. I'm sure we'll be busy today. You know how curious the public is."

Mark shook his head. "No. This'll get me started, and yes, I do know." He glanced down at the list. "By the way, did you know Devin Burke?"

"No. Not really."

Mark tilted his head.

The short man, who couldn't weigh more than a hundred thirty pounds soaking wet, leaned back against the paper-covered desk. "Well, you know, you see people, but that doesn't mean you know them. Never noticed him until a few months ago, and then I started seeing him daily, right before I left." Steve stood and opened the door for Mark, reminding him subtly that he needed to leave. He locked the door behind them, and then continued, "I stick mostly to the dayshift. Lunch is our busiest time, and between my night manager and the bartender, they pretty much take care of things. Devin started showing up around happy hour. The only reason I recognized him was because he sat in the same spot and was always talking to Ashlyn, my night bartender."

"Were they dating?"

The man laughed. "Well, I don't follow my employees' personal lives, but yeah, there was something there, I'd guess."

Mark nodded, appreciative to get his first lead. He extended his hand. "Thank you for your time, Mr. Baxter. I'll replace the tape."

The man waved him off. "Don't worry about it. I have some unopened ones."

"One last question if you don't mind. Do you happen to have the bartender's phone number?" Obviously, she would be the first person he needed to question.

"Sure, I have Ashlyn's number right here." The man removed his phone from his pocket, clicked through a couple of keys, then read out the number.

Mark wrote the digits beside her name from yesterday's schedule. How convenient. Ashlyn worked last night.

CHAPTER 5

Ashlyn listened to the voicemail message from Detective Mark Waters for the tenth time before walking into her statistics class. As she eased herself into her chair, she flipped her phone to silent mode. The professor immediately started teaching, but his words drifted through the air without penetrating her thoughts. Maybe some of it would seep into her brain because all she could do was replay the detective's message in her head over and over, attempting to decipher if he suspected she was responsible for Devin's death.

She turned toward the rectangular window that offered a spectacular view of the college's common area, wishing she could appreciate the beauty of the blooming Yoshino and Kwanzan cherry trees with their pure-white and bright-pink blossoms. Pennsylvania in the springtime was like a tiny miracle every year. She always longed for the dark and dreary days of winter to cease, replaced by the vibrant colors of spring. She'd researched all the names of the trees she loved and added them to her design notepad of how she'd decorate her estate one day. She would make sure that her property had trees that were green year-round, interspersed with shrubs, flowers, and trees that bloomed at different intervals throughout the year, so her view would always be cheerful.

Now, her dreams of the perfect business, house, and life felt as though they would wither and die.

Inserting one of her earbuds, she decided to listen to the detective's message one more time before deciding what to do.

> *Ms. Allan, this is Detective Mark Waters with Edenbury Police Department. I'm investigating the death of Devin Burke and would like to ask you a few questions. Please call me to set up a time that you can come into the station.*

He left his office number and cell phone number,

stating that she could reach him day or night at one of those numbers.

Tugging her turtleneck sweater around her chin self-consciously, she swiped away a tear. It hadn't been her fault; she'd been protecting herself. She didn't even understand exactly how it had happened. One minute Devin was hurting her, and she had defended herself with the only weapon she had, and the next he was dead.

She twisted a strand of her hair, resisting the urge to chew on it as she'd done as a child. Her mother would always slap her hand from her face, telling her to be a lady. Just as she'd done when she'd tried to replace the hair with her fingernail. Her mother had reiterated that if she wanted to be anything in life, she needed to use what the Good Lord had given her. All of it. Her intelligence coupled with her looks and body would take her wherever she wanted to go, her mother would tell her.

Ashlyn released a sigh. The only place she might be going now is prison.

No, she reprimanded herself internally. The detective simply wanted to ask her questions. There was nothing proving that she'd had any part in Devin's death. *Nothing but the tape, that is*, she reminded herself.

She needed to see what was on the tape. But between school and work, she wouldn't be able to watch it until late tonight.

In order not to look guilty, she'd decided not to stay home from school or work today. To go on with her life as if she hadn't heard anything had happened to her ex-boyfriend, since Devin had made it clear on her voicemail a few weeks ago that he no longer wanted to see her. The only reason he'd even come into the restaurant last night was because of what she'd told him on the phone. She'd started with, "F*ine! I don't ever want to see you either.*" She'd learned a long time ago never to fall on her knees and beg for anything. Men viewed that as weakness. If she acted as if she didn't care, she'd have a better chance of winning him back. But then she'd said the words that had really ticked him off. She'd told him, "*And no, I won't be having an abortion.*"

CHAPTER 6

Leaning back in his office chair, Mark clicked *play* on the antiquated system to watch the security feed. Who used tape anymore? Most businesses had gone to digital. Instead of watching the entire day, Mark fast-forwarded to about an hour before closing time, assuming whatever had happened that made Devin Burke commit suicide, happened before the bar closed, or directly afterward.

Six people sat around the bar, two couples, and two single men, no one resembling Burke's description, even before he'd become bird food.

A woman stepped out of the ladies' room, and Mark inclined forward. She was breathtaking. Long light hair restrained by a small clip fell around her shoulders. Since the image was black and white, he couldn't be sure if she had blond or strawberry-blond hair, but based on the sprinkling of freckles across the bridge of her nose, his bet was on strawberry blond. The woman stepped behind the bar as she dabbed at her eyes and then threw the tissue in the garbage.

Ashlyn Allan? he wondered.

She looked like an Ashlyn. But why did the first woman who'd caught his attention outside of work have to be one he had to interrogate? Of course, it wasn't her fault that the guy she'd been most likely dating had jumped in front of a train. At least he hoped not.

Mark rested his chin on his clasped hands as he watched the bartender tally the tabs for the customers. In between the patrons finishing their drinks and paying their bills, she hand washed glasses in the sink, wiped down liquor bottles, and put juices and cut fruit in a small fridge under the counter.

After she'd escorted the last customer to the door, she threw her hands over her face, and her body wracked from what appeared to be her sobbing. Mark tilted his head in confusion. She'd seemed so together only seconds earlier. Clearly she had been putting on a show in front of her customers.

The Library

She dried her tears with a tissue that she pulled out of her apron, then lifted her phone to her ear. Within seconds, she started pacing the area behind the bar, stopping only when she opened the cash register. She shoved all the money inside a bank bag, then resumed her pacing. Mark could see that she was having an argument. She threw her free hand in the air as if disgusted with the person on the other end of the line. A second later, she glared down at the phone as if she'd lost the connection.

After she stuffed the phone in her apron, she snatched her purse from under the counter and disappeared up the service steps that led to the upstairs portion of the restaurant, the area where Mark had been in the office.

Mark waited a few minutes, noticing how ghostly-looking the bar was without people. The plants swayed lightly as they had done the previous night when Mark had been investigating the murder.

He stopped the tape.

If the train had already passed, the man had already jumped, and he'd be dead. Mark rewound the tape, concentrating on the scenes from different camera angles. The kitchen and front door feeds were blank, so no sensors had been tripped. He watched the shed area overlooking the train tracks. The tape was moving, so the train's approach must have tripped it because nothing moved or caught his eye. Just a barren field behind the building with a shed and a few buckets and bags of trash. He waited a few seconds, and then, there it was. The train. Nothing else appeared in the scene.

His eyes darted to the left-hand side of the screen after the train had passed. The plants swayed as he'd noticed before. After a few minutes, the bartender came down the stairs, her head lowered as though she was still upset. She made her way toward the front entrance, unlocked the door, turned off the lights, and then left the building.

Nothing changed in the four-square scene on his screen. He pressed *fast-forward*, but still nothing changed. And then the screen went blank where nothing had been recorded. He fast-forwarded until the end of the tape, but nothing else appeared, which was impossible.

There should have been something else on the tape even if Devin never stepped inside the bar before or after it closed. He should have seen himself, Townsend, and the forensic team. But they weren't there.

The manager had given him the wrong one. This was not last night's tape.

CHAPTER 7

Deciding she'd ignore the detective's message, Ashlyn went directly to work after school, stopping long enough to grab a double-shot latte from Starbucks so she wouldn't fall asleep halfway through her shift. She'd call him in the middle of happy hour, when the bar was buzzin'. That way it'd be too loud to hear, and she'd have to call him later. Preferably, after she pulled herself together.

When she got to work, she went straight to the ladies' room. As she suspected, she had black circles under her eyes from lack of sleep. She opened her makeup bag and dabbed a few dots of concealer under her eyes, touched up her face with some powder, and brushed a hint of blush over her cheeks to make her face appear cheerful and healthy, even if she wasn't. Lastly, she dabbed on some lip-gloss.

She appraised her perfectly flat belly, which would be round with life in a few months. How could she do this on her own? All her dreams. She might as well flush them down the toilet. Would Devin's parents be interested in the child of the woman they didn't even know existed? No. She couldn't tell them. Right after they blamed her for their son's death, they'd probably try to take her child. Her mother wouldn't help. In fact, she'd chastise her for being irresponsible.

It wasn't as if they hadn't used protection; they had. Every time. It wasn't her fault the condom broke. Even though Devin had claimed it was her fault because she should have been on the pill. The fact was she wasn't on the pill because she didn't sleep around. She'd waited until she found the man whom she'd thought could make her dreams come true. All of her dreams of life — and love. Stupid, stupid, stupid! Never again.

She placed her hand over her tummy. *Never again*, she recited to her unborn child. *I will have you, and I'll do it on my own.* She didn't need a man to make her dreams come true, as Momma had always pounded into her brain. "*I'll* make my dreams come true, dammit!" she said aloud, but then blanched when the door opened.

Ashlyn sucked in a breath and took a long look at her face in the mirror. *I'll graduate before the baby is born. I'll start looking for a job now before I start showing, and I'll make it happen*, she said to herself this time.

She pushed open the door and stepped out, ready to work.

The daytime bartender glanced at her, but didn't smile. Instead, a look of sadness washed over her face. "I'm so sorry," Corrine said, walking toward her. "I could cover your shift if you need me."

Ashlyn hung her head. "No. I'm fine. I have to work."

Corrine bit her bottom lip. "Do you know why he did it?"

"No. And honestly, Corrine, I don't feel like talking about this. Could you keep this on the down-low? You're the only one who knows I was dating Devin. I'd rather not have the media harassing me."

The tall brunette dragged Ashlyn to the side and whispered in her ear. "Well, they'll still probably harass you. Different agencies were here all day. When Steve kicked them out, they returned, but as customers. They'd sit and not say anything, then they would subtly start asking questions, usually right after a big tip. At least that part was nice."

Ashlyn huffed out a breath. That was all she needed.

"Really, if you want me to work, I will."

"No." She inhaled another deep breath. "I'd just be home moping."

"Okay, hon. Lemme know. I'll cash out then." Corrine stepped behind the bar and closed out her register.

Ashlyn spent the next few minutes putting on a happy face, answering all her regulars' comments: *Can you believe it? Did you know him? Wow, what would make a good-looking boy like that kill himself?*

Yeah, she wondered. *Why would he?* Had she hit him harder than she thought? She shook off the feelings and made herself busy cutting fruit for the evening, twirling cocktail napkins, and checking her back-ups of juices and sour mixes.

"Hey, Ash," Steve called to her from the end of the bar as she was half buried beneath the counter.

She pulled herself upright and walked toward her boss. "Yeah?"

He nudged her around the bar. "Did the detective call you?"

She gulped. "Um ... yeah, but I was too busy with school. I'll call him when I'm not busy."

"Okay. Do you know why —"

"No!" she said too loudly. "Why would I have any idea?"

He tilted his head, narrowing his eyes at her. "Ash, I know you were seeing him."

"Oh, God." She dropped her head, wondering if he'd told the police.

"The detective who came by earlier asked for your number," he continued.

She squeezed her eyes shut, silently praying that he hadn't said anything to the police. "Did you tell him Devin and I were dating?"

"I said I suspected. Are you okay?"

She waved him off. "Fine. I have to work." She walked behind the bar, attempting to push everything to the recesses of her mind. Of course, if she couldn't do it in statistics, how would she do it in a job where she practically moved around like a robot? She turned around, as if in a daze, and noticed Steve hadn't left. She narrowed her eyes at him. The last thing she needed was her boss to think she couldn't handle her position.

"Okay," Steve said. "I'm heading home, then. Call me if you need me to cover your shift."

She definitely couldn't afford to lose any shifts with a baby on the way. *A baby.* She shook the thoughts out of her head. *Just concentrate on work.*

Corrine was right; the restaurant buzzed with business. And for a little while, she was able to push Devin out of her thoughts. Until a group of barely-legal college kids sitting in one of the booths in the bar area started hammering her for details, that is. She politely ignored their queries, and eventually, they stopped asking.

As she turned away from the students, she noticed a gentleman had taken residence at the table in the corner. Rarely did anyone sit there because it was dark. There were no windows, and supporting columns blocked the TV screens, so customers couldn't watch whatever sport was in season. In fact, the only people who usually sat there were employees.

"Hello." She forced a smile as she approached him.

The man smiled in response as he closed his menu, and Ashlyn couldn't help but notice her smile morphed into an authentic smile. He was cuter than cute and dressed impeccably.

"Can I get you something to drink?"

"Just water —" He paused. "On second thought, do you know how to make a Lynchburg Lemonade?"

Another smile lifted her cheeks. "Of course. Would you like something to eat too? I noticed you were looking at the menu?"

"Can I eat here?" he asked.

"Sure. Most single men —" She peeked down at his hand. "I mean, most single diners eat at the bar."

"I better eat then. I haven't eaten anything all day. I'll take the Depot burger, but no fries. Can you substitute a salad or vegetable?"

She laughed. "Yep. Let me guess, vinaigrette dressing?"

He nodded, and she glided off, shaking her hips a little more than necessary. And then she mentally wanted to slap herself. Hadn't she told herself that she didn't need to look for a man? Especially after what had happened to her last night. But this guy appeared perfect. His clothes screamed money or possibly just good taste. Even his stance demanded attention. And he was so cute. Shorter hair than she was accustomed, but the dark brown hair with a hint of curl set off his deep green eyes. Greener eyes than she'd ever imagined possible. His shoulders were wide, but he wasn't bulky. She appreciated a man who kept his body in tiptop shape. And skipping the fries, but keeping the hamburger said that he didn't deny himself what he wanted; he simply made choices and had self-discipline.

Ashlyn keyed his order into the computer and grabbed a salad out of the cooler, along with a ramekin of vinaigrette on the side. She delivered the salad to his table, then reached behind the bar for her basket of rolled silverware and condiments. She set the items on the table. "I'll be right back with your drink."

Normal servers would get a customer's drink order first. But when she was out of the bar area, taking food orders, it was easier to get it all at once. Otherwise, she'd be stuck behind the bar. After making the Jack Daniel's style lemonade and setting it in front of the handsome stranger, she remembered she needed to call the detective. She'd call his office number. That way, maybe he'd be gone for the day. She took out her phone and searched for the number she'd saved so she would know if he called again.

The call went directly to voicemail. She stooped down behind the bar as though she were reaching for something and cupped her hand over the phone to mask her words. "Detective Waters, this is Ashlyn Allan. I had school, and now I'm at work, so I'll call you tomorrow." She clicked *end* before she could say anything stupid. Her best bet was to act as if she had nothing to hide.

She straightened her body, smoothed her apron, and shot a glance around the bar. The good-looking man at her table was watching her. Feeling paranoid for no reason, she smiled and hurried to see if she could help anyone else.

CHAPTER 8

Mark watched as Ashlyn flitted around the bar, doing everything she could to avoid eye contact with him, it seemed. Had she known he was the man she'd called? She couldn't have. When she'd returned her eyes to him, though, her eyes had darted away as if flustered.

He'd caught her comment and glance at his left hand when he'd asked about food. He didn't know how he felt about a woman flirting with a man the night after her boyfriend committed suicide. Then again, she flirted for a living. Her job counted on her being good at what she did, but it also required that she be friendly and flirty.

Unfortunately for him, as he'd suspected earlier, Ashlyn was an absolute knockout. He'd been correct about the hair too. Just a hint of strawberry tint in those long blond curls, that for some reason he had an overwhelming desire to run his fingers through.

Forcing his mind to the current situation, as he always did, his thoughts returned to his *jumper*. Why would a twenty-five-year-old man, who he'd now verified had no money issues, a job waiting as Daddy's CEO next month, and a hot girlfriend to boot, jump in front of a train? Ashlyn wasn't a big enough girl to have pushed him. Burke was six-two and one-ninety according to the coroner. Ashlyn couldn't be more than five-six and a hundred twenty pounds fully dressed. He shook his head as he imagined her body without being fully dressed.

Ashlyn stepped to the table with a plate in her hand. "I went ahead and gave you a baked potato with your burger. It was all lonely by itself." She set his dinner in front of him. "Can I get you anything else?"

Lonely indeed, he thought, still attempting to remove Ashlyn's naked image, which was now keeping *him* company. "A-1 and one more of these, please." He pointed to his drink.

She nodded and strolled behind the bar, returning a few seconds later with the bottle of steak sauce and another spiked lemonade. "Enjoy. Holler if you need anything else."

He smiled as he watched her walk away. A nice view. As he ate, he observed everything she did. She stayed busy, but the few times she had downtime, he saw her fall into a trance, and even watched her wipe away a tear. So she wasn't heartless; she was merely trying to work through the pain. He'd known that feeling far too many times. He recalled the video he'd watched earlier, how she'd been smiling and waving, and then her body had wracked with pain. He'd wanted to reach through the screen and hold her. Of course, he'd also wanted to know who was responsible for giving him the wrong tape. And since he didn't think they were simply going to hand over the correct one, he decided the better path would be to do a little investigating.

Normally he wouldn't drink, but hey, this was off-the-clock investigating. The captain wanted answers, but it didn't mean the city would front overtime pay for those answers. Nope! They'd expect him to find those answers during his 8-4 shift.

After he'd finished his meal, Ashlyn cleared his plate. But since he was still sipping on the same drink, she didn't offer a refill. Mark sat and watched as the restaurant filled and emptied several times. Ashlyn came by and made small talk a few times, brought him another drink, but then carried on with her duties.

Around eleven, there were only a few people sitting around the bar and a couple of servers finishing their tables. The beautiful strawberry-blonde returned to his table, and this time, sat down across from him. "So why haven't I seen you here before? Are you new to the area?"

"No. I usually come by at lunch. I know the owner, Steve," he said, hoping she'd be a little more at ease that he wasn't some stalker, even though in a way, he was.

"Oh. Cool! Steve's awesome. I've worked for him for three years. It's great work while I finish my undergrad."

He nodded. Even though he'd known most of that. He'd already done a background check. She'd never been in trouble, not even a speeding ticket, even driving a turbocharged Jetta.

"What's your major?" he asked.

She smiled, and he enjoyed the slight flush in her cheeks. "Business. I figure it's the most versatile. Whether I want to open my own business, run somebody else's, or even teach, it's a great degree."

"I agree."

"What do you do?" she asked.

Mark inspected the Gucci watch on her wrist, the diamond tennis bracelet on the other, her Lucky You jeans, and the eight-hundred-dollar biker boots she tended bar in, and smiled. Either she came from money, or she made sure she looked like it. She'd have no interest in a police detective. Although he did well with his other ventures, he couldn't keep her in the style she was accustomed to. But for some reason, he'd wanted to believe that he could, so he decided to tell a half-lie, especially since he didn't want her to know he was here to observe her, hoping he'd get some insight on what happened last night.

"I have several ventures," he said, which was true.

She stood up, dismissing him, making her way to the bar. She swapped coasters, replaced a few drinks, closed out another patron's tab, and then found her way back to him.

She dropped down in the chair again. "Okay ... another question, since you obviously didn't want to answer the last one. Why are you still here?" she asked point-blank. "You've never been here at night that I've seen, and suddenly, you've spent your entire evening at this tiny table. You can't even see the TV."

He smiled, wondering who the detective was. She was smart. He lifted his iPhone as an answer. "Fruit Ninja."

She narrowed her eyes. "You've been playing games all night? And here I thought maybe you were interested in me, but I wasn't sure if I needed to call my big brother to escort me to my car."

"Do you have a big brother that comes and does that?" Slipping into detective mode, he wondered. A boyfriend had her bawling the night before, and then maybe big brother shows up the next night. That could work.

"No." She shrugged. "I don't have any siblings."

"Oh." He exhaled a breath of relief at that, but it also meant he was back to square one. "Well, I assure you, you don't have to worry about me. I'm just chillin' … for the first time in a long time actually."

"You want another drink, then?"

"Might as well. I already have to call a taxi."

"Oh, I could —"

"Ash!" called out a glassy-eyed man at the end of the bar. The big guy had his arm and half his body draped over a tiny woman next to him. "Close me out, will ya?"

Mark hoped the woman was driving.

The Library

Ashlyn waved in the man's direction, fixed Mark his drink and set it before him, and then skipped over to the mismatched couple.

Now Mark and Ashlyn were the last two people in the bar. It appeared all the kitchen staff had left as well. She ambled back to his table and slid down across from him again.

"Do you close by yourself every night?" he asked. "That seems awfully dangerous."

She reached into her apron and pulled out a bottle of OC spray. "I used to keep it behind the bar; now I've decided to keep it on me. I know it's not a failsafe, but I figure it'll do the trick."

"It definitely will." He leaned over the small round table that kept them two feet apart. He'd downed a few too many drinks, but man, they went down smoothly. But now he didn't like what he was thinking. "So now what?"

"Well," Ashlyn said, "the old saying in the restaurant business is: If you've got time to lean, you've got time to clean. The bar rarely stays empty long. But if it does, I always have something that needs cleaning in this old place."

Mark laughed. She wanted to clean, and he wanted

to spin her across the wood floors. "You guys play music?"

She nodded. "Sure. What kind?"

"Something slow."

While she moved to the bar and messed with the remote control for the TV, switching the sports channel to the music channel, he moved to the farthest stool at the end of the bar.

When she turned, she gasped, throwing her hand over her mouth. "Oh!" She dropped her hand and shook her head as if trying to shake off what had scared her. But her eyes glazed over.

Something inside Mark churned, and he immediately felt something for this woman. "I'm sorry. Did I do something wrong?"

"No." She shook her head again, exhaling a whoosh of air. "It's just ... you looked like ..."

"A ghost?" he asked, trying to lighten the situation. "I heard you have ghosts?" He let out a half-laugh, and she nodded.

"Yeah." She inhaled another breath as though she was trying to get her bearings.

"Wanna dance?" he asked quickly, before she turned away from him and started cleaning the bar as she'd mentioned.

The Library

"I couldn't possibly. What if —"

He stepped around the side of the bar, took her hand, and pulled her out to the center of the floor. "*What if*," he repeated. "It's not as though you're dancing on the bar. I told you ... tonight's the first time I've relaxed in a long time, even though I should be working." He twirled her out once and pulled her back. "But you're so darn beautiful."

She huffed out a breath as if she didn't believe him. "What type of work should you be doing instead of playing games on your iPhone and dancing with a stranger?"

He sighed. "I interview people."

She scrunched her eyebrows together. "What does that mean?"

"I find out if people are telling the truth."

She stopped moving and tried to pull back. "Don't pull away yet, Ashlyn."

Her eyes filled. "You're scaring me. I don't even know your name. And you're asking me to dance, and acting all strange. Who are you?"

"I swear I won't hurt you. Keep your hand on the pepper spray if you like." He smiled and drew her closer. With her boots, she was the perfect height that he could tilt his head and kiss those shiny pink lips that intensified the hint of strawberry in her hair, but then she'd really freak out. And then she would freak out again when she figured out who he was. "Just dance with me for a few more minutes. Tell me about your ghosts," he whispered in her ear. He inhaled the spicy scent of her perfume. It suited her. No flowery smell; it was fiery like her. The song changed, and she retracted again, as if to end the dance. "One more, please," he requested with a slow smile.

She laughed nervously, seeming to relax in his arms. "We do have ghosts. In fact, Edda was my great-grandmother."

"Edda?"

"You haven't heard the stories?"

He raised an eyebrow. "Should I have?"

"If you live around here, most people have. At the time, the death of Edda Barrett was the most gruesome murder on record in this area. A man discovered her when he saw buzzards flying around her remains. She had nothing on but a shredded dress, her fingertips had been practically cut off, half of her jaw had been knocked out, and if that wasn't enough, the murderer lit her on fire and dumped her in the river. Evidently she'd been seeing —" Ashlyn clasped her hands over her mouth, and then pulled away, darting to the bathroom. "Oh, my God!" she screamed as she entered the tiny room, the door slamming behind her.

CHAPTER 9

Ashlyn leaned over the toilet and expelled what remained of her lunch while the man knocked on the door.

"Ashlyn, are you okay?"

She grabbed a handful of toilet paper and wiped her lips and then moved to the sink and washed out her mouth the best she could. Well, at least she wouldn't be tempted to kiss the stranger, as she'd been when he was holding her.

Gawking at her image in the mirror, she almost expected to see her great-grandmother's dead face glowering at her. She had heard all the stories, but she'd never seen Edda's ghost. But the feeling that washed over her, the same feeling she'd had yesterday when Devin had attacked her, unnerved her. The déjà vu feeling made sense. Her great-grandmother had been brutally murdered by her boyfriend who was reportedly angry because she'd had his baby without him knowing while he was away at school. According to Ashlyn's grandmother, who'd heard the story from her grandmother, Edda was supposed to drive to the boy's parents and meet them for the first time. Edda had called her mother with exciting news, saying she was getting married and that she'd have a grand wedding. She hadn't even told her parents who the boy was because he had wanted to make sure he told his parents privately.

The stranger knocked on the door again. "Are you okay?"

"Yes. Just nauseated. Give me a second, please."

"Okay," he said from behind the door.

She stopped hyperventilating and focused her thoughts on the man outside the door. He seemed like a nice enough guy. If he'd wanted to rape her, he surely could have by now.

Ashlyn stared into the mirror again. Her situation was almost exactly the same as what her great-grandmother had experienced. Devin had been mad enough that he might have killed her. As it was, he'd tried to choke her to death, but she'd fought back. Not that it had stopped him. Even after she'd hit him over the head with a liquor bottle, he'd not released her.

She'd always seen in movies where the bottle would break. She probably hadn't smacked him hard enough. But then —

A knock interrupted her contemplations. "There's a group of people out here," the man called.

"Okay. Tell them I'll be right there."

She washed out her mouth again, used some tissue to dab the smeared mascara from under her eyes, and left the restroom, walking directly to the stranger. "What's your name?" she demanded.

He looked like a puppy who'd been slapped on the nose. "You have customers."

She turned and waved. "Hey, guys. I'll be right there."

"No problem," Jeff, the tallest member of the group shouted, jumping onto a stool at the opposite end of the bar. The nurses came in several times a week. They worked three twelve-hour shifts a week, so when they worked the twelve-to-twelve shifts, they swung by before last call.

Ashlyn turned to him, her hands on her hips. "Who are you?"

The Library

He released a long breath. "Promise you won't be furious? That you'll give me a chance to explain, understand that I'm trying to help."

She narrowed her eyes. "How can I promise that?"

"Take care of your customers and then come talk to me, okay?"

It didn't take a rocket scientist to figure out what was going on. "Okay ... *Mark* ..." she ventured, watching as his face relaxed. Who else could he be? It still ticked her off that he was trying to get information from her underhandedly. But technically, he hadn't asked her anything about Devin's death, so maybe he was just observing her, making certain she wasn't guilty. But what if she was? What if her hitting Devin on the head had knocked something loose in his brain, causing him to race out the door?

"Last call, guys," she informed her regulars as she approached.

Their laughing and carrying on stopped as their faces fell. Jeff leaned his long body over the bar. "It's only 12:15. We got forty-five minutes, sweetheart."

"Not tonight, Jeff. Sorry. I have an emergency."

Jeff flashed a look over her head. "Everything okay? That's not the normal guy. Although, he looks friendlier. That other guy who was here every night always had a scowl on his face."

"I'm fine, but really, I gotta close down the place."

The rest of the group whined and moaned, but they'd just head down the road to Aggie's Tavern.

Ashlyn followed the group of nurses to the door, turned off the *open* sign, and then locked the door behind them. When she turned, Mark — at least she assumed his name was Mark — was right behind her.

"I guess our dance is over." He released a nervous laugh. "And yes, I'm Mark. But honestly, I meant no harm."

"Do I need an attorney?"

"I don't know, do you? I'm not here to arrest you. I'm here because I saw the tape."

She narrowed her eyes in confusion.

"Not last night's tape, the previous night. I saw how upset you were."

"I didn't kill him —"

"Shh ..." He stepped forward. "I'm not on duty, and I'm not interviewing you."

She gulped, wondering why she felt such an attraction to this man whom she didn't even know. Instinctively, she licked her lips as he leaned forward, but then remembering, she jerked her head to the side. "No! I need to brush my teeth."

He stopped his forward motion and smiled. "Oh yeah. I forgot about that. I guess I need to call a taxi anyway."

"I'll drive you home," she offered. "I mean ... you're a cop, right?"

"Detective."

She tilted her head. "You don't look like a detective."

"Thank God!" He laughed.

"Give me a second. I have to put away my money." She gathered her stuff from behind the bar, threw the money from her drawer in a bank bag, and ran upstairs. It'd never creeped her out to go upstairs alone before. But realizing that what had happened to her great-grandmother could have happened to her, she felt an unnerving chill sweep through her body as she made her way up the dark stairwell to the office. The Depot had been the last place Edda had been seen alive. Some customers had claimed to feel as if they were being choked. She wondered if the man who'd killed Edda had choked her as Devin had tried to kill her last night. Maybe the feelings Edda had were now felt by others who were sensitive. She was flesh and blood to Edda, though, and she'd never felt anything.

Ashlyn locked up her money and ran downstairs to where Mark stood by the door. She'd never dated a detective before. She'd always set her sights on businessmen. Some women wanted a doctor or a lawyer, but she'd done her homework. Unless they were specialists or owned a firm, they weren't wealthy, and they worked too many hours. Whereas a businessman, real-estate developer, or construction company owner owned their business, could make their own hours, and there was no ceiling to what she could help turn the business into. But now that she regarded the handsome man leaning against the door, she couldn't see any of that. She just saw *him* and how even though he didn't know her but a few hours, he'd wanted to comfort her when she'd been scared. Somehow, that presented a better future than money could ever buy. Her mother had been wrong; she'd been wrong.

CHAPTER 10

Ashlyn knew she was probably crazy, but for some reason, she trusted Mark. Instead of driving him home, she drove toward her apartment. When she passed the street he'd told her to turn down, she saw him lean forward out of her peripherals, but he didn't ask. She felt his gaze as it seared her, as he had done when he'd held her in his arms, before she'd rushed to the ladies' room.

She cast him a quick glance. "I have to brush my teeth."

He laughed. "I have an extra toothbrush. You could've asked."

"Yeah, but there's something I need to show you." She needed to show him the tape. She was sure the tape would prove her innocence. After all, she'd struck Devin in self-defense.

Mark didn't comment, and she wondered if he was thinking the same thing she was. Probably not. He was a man, after all.

She hit the far-right remote on the visor and the gate opened to her complex. After winding along the tree-lined road and around the first set of townhomes, she hung a right onto her private driveway. She pushed the other remote, and the garage opened.

"Nice place," Mark commented. "You're not dealing, are you?"

Knowing he was joking, she laughed. "I save every penny I make." He nodded in appreciation, apparently not used to a woman saying that.

Ashlyn ascended the stairs leading to her townhouse. The entire bottom floor was a garage with the living area on the second floor and the bedrooms on the third floor.

"Safe place," were Mark's only words as they climbed the steps.

"It is. The stairs can be a bear when I'm bringing in groceries, but at least I don't have to worry about someone crawling in my bedroom window." No ... she'd known her attacker. Even though they'd been broken up for weeks. The only reason she'd called him was because she'd discovered she was pregnant.

"Exactly. Never good to have your bedroom on a ground floor."

She unlocked the main door and escorted Mark to the living room, then opened up the balcony doors. "Make yourself at home. If you want another drink, I have wine in the fridge." She dashed up the stairs before he could comment. She should feel nervous having a complete stranger in her house, but oddly, she felt more at ease with him than any other man she'd brought here, including Devin. She decided to rinse off the grime of the day and brush her teeth in the shower so she'd be quick. It took her less than three minutes, and she was in her room, slipping into something more comfortable, her plush Victoria's Secret sweatshirt and sweatpants. Comfortably dressed, she sauntered down the stairs. Now, she needed to work up the nerve to show him the tape. But first he needed to hear her side of the story.

Mark held a glass of wine in his hand, and another glass sat on the coffee table. Setting his glass down, he stood as she entered the room and closed the distance between them. Wasting no time, he pulled her into his arms, and Ashlyn couldn't help but feel completely at ease with his advance. She wanted it, longed for it even. Desire surged through her body, tingling all the way to her fingertips. She wanted him. But there was still something they should be doing instead, the reason she'd brought him here. But — *it could wait*, she thought as his eyes gobbled her up. Not in a lustful way, but a passion, a mutual fire that burned between them, as if they were supposed to meet.

He moved his hand under her chin, nudging it slightly. His other hand found the clip in her hair. He removed it, dropping it on the table. As he combed his fingers through her hair, he pulled her tighter against his broad chest. Her heart thrashed so wildly in anticipation of his kiss that she was sure he'd hear it. He covered her mouth with his, smoothly parting her lips. His tongue expertly explored with gentle precision, as if finding its way and unlocking the entry to her soul. She tasted the chardonnay on his tongue and wanted more — of him. The wine could wait.

Her legs felt weak, and she was certain if his arms weren't around her, she'd melt through the floor. She inched her fingers up his chest, wrapping her hands around his neck, wondering where this man had been the last few years. She'd never felt so much passion in a kiss.

The Library

Mark led her to the sofa, never breaking the kiss. He supported her body against the backrest as he continued to kiss her, running his fingers down the side of her face, her neck, and across her collarbone.

He finally broke the kiss, but only to move to her ear. "You are beautiful, Ashlyn. And so sexy." He moved lower, his mouth nibbling its way down the side of her neck, tugging on her collar so he could kiss her fully.

She threw her head back at the feel of his warm lips on her skin. "Oh, that feels so good." And it did. No one had ever kissed her with such passion, such fervor.

He bolted upright. "Oh dear Lord, Ashlyn."

She sat straight, pulling the top of her sweatshirt higher around her neck. She'd forgotten.

"What on earth happened?" Mark reached toward her, and she tried to move away, but she was trapped between him and the arm of the sofa. "He did this to you, didn't he?"

She gulped, and tears poured down her face as she nodded her answer.

Mark lifted his hand again, as if asking permission. "May I?"

Unable to speak because of the tears strangling her voice, she nodded again.

He lifted her chin to reveal the marks she'd tried to cover. Shaking his head, he ran his hand across his forehead. "Please tell me what happened. I'm not on duty, and I want to help you."

"I'm scared."

CHAPTER 11

Mark lifted Ashlyn's hands. "I know. If you did anything, stop right now, and we'll find an attorney. But if you had nothing to do with his death, talk to me."

She shook her head, but he wasn't sure what that meant.

Why did she have to be the first woman he'd felt something for in three years? "He hurt you?"

She nodded again.

"Why?"

She shook her head as her face puckered, not wanting to tell him, it seemed. "I'm pregnant."

"Oh."

She nodded again. "Yep. That was his response

until I told him I wouldn't get rid of the baby." She gasped for air. "He came in last night, right before closing. After everyone left, he grabbed me and shook me, demanding that he couldn't ruin his life because of me ..."

Mark squeezed her hands, encouraging her. She obviously wasn't guilty, or she wouldn't be talking.

"He screamed at me," she continued. "He told me he'd pay me a hundred thousand dollars if I had an abortion. I knew then that money meant nothing to me. I wouldn't kill my unborn child for money. So when I still refused, he started choking me."

She dropped her head to her chest.

Mark nudged up her chin. "What happened?"

"I grabbed the only thing I could. A bottle of liquor. I hit him with it. But it didn't break, and he kept coming. He knocked me against the bar and continued to choke me, and then he was gone." Ashlyn shook her head. "I don't know if I blacked out, but when I felt his grip release, I struggled to my feet and saw him running out the rear exit. Maybe he assumed I was dead ..." Tears streamed down her face again. "I ran after him and I ... I saw him run in front of the train, but I closed my eyes, knowing what would happen.

THE LIBRARY

Then not knowing what to do, I panicked. I grabbed my stuff and got out of there as fast as I could."

Mark gazed into her eyes, realizing she'd told him the entire truth.

"Could my hitting him have caused that — caused him to run like that?" she choked out.

"You had every right to defend yourself, Ashlyn. But you said he kept coming, so obviously you didn't hit him hard enough." Mark pressed his hand against her cheek. "Where's the tape? It'll obviously clear you."

She sucked in a deep breath and whooshed it out. Standing up on obviously wobbly legs, she trudged over to her purse. "I have an old VCR player upstairs."

Mark stood. "Let's go."

He followed Ashlyn to her bedroom, admiring that she'd decorated it in different shades of cream and mauve. An antique-looking bed with an eyelet coverlet was the focal point of her master bedroom. His mother would love it; she was such a romantic at heart.

Ashlyn handed him the tape, pointing to the VCR player on her dresser. "I know it's weird to have a VCR player since the Blu-ray discs are so much better, but I always loved fairy tales. I still watch my old childhood animated Disney movies on VCR tapes. *Beauty and the Beast* and *The Little Mermaid* are my favorites."

Mark smiled and pointed to himself. "*Aladdin* and *Lion King*."

He walked over to the dresser and put the tape in the slot. He fast-forwarded the tape until he saw the scene. He turned to her sitting on the bed. "You shouldn't watch this."

She nodded, burying her head into one of the lace-covered throw pillows.

Mark hit *play* and then stood in front of the small TV, blocking her view in the event she got the urge to look. It was one thing being attacked. It was another to watch it. He'd seen women break into violent tears after viewing their attacks that had been caught on security cameras. One woman had actually been raped in an elevator in between floors. *Sickos*, he thought.

He continued to watch the video, seeing the events play out exactly as she'd described. But then he recoiled at an image she hadn't described, a gasp escaping his throat.

The bed squeaked as Ashlyn must have jumped up, appearing at his side at the same time the recording showed Devin Burke darting out of the building, her following him a few seconds later. Mark stood there with his hand over his mouth, not believing what he'd seen.

"What was it?" Ashlyn shrieked. "What did you see?"

He turned to her, feeling the blood rush through his body as his heart pounded out a vicious rhythm. "You weren't to blame, Ashlyn." He ran his hands through his hair, willing his heart to slow so he could speak, wondering if he should tell her. The image he saw was clear; he hadn't imagined it. Now he understood what had made Devin run in fear.

Ashlyn's eyes grew round as she stared at him, waiting for an answer. "What did you see, Mark?"

There was no way to describe what he saw, but he knew *whom* he saw. "Your great-grandmother."

This is the end of part one, *The Depot*, but read on for the second part of the story, which begins six months later in *The Library*.

Part Two

The Library
(Where Life Checks Out)

PROLOGUE

Wade Buchanan inserted his key into the deadbolt of his front door the same time he did every night. Only this time, the door glided open as though some unseen force had invited him inside. The house was quiet. Too quiet. Usually he'd hear the sound of the TV, a kitchen timer alerting that dinner was ready, or the constant boom from the stereo upstairs. But this evening, tomblike silence greeted him.

His wife had threatened to leave; he just hadn't believed her. After all, she'd been grumbling that same nonsense for twenty-two years. A romantic getaway for two would straighten her out.

Their only child was going off to grad school in a few weeks. So for the first time in their marriage, they'd be childless. His life had changed the night she told him she was pregnant two weeks away from high school graduation, but it hadn't stopped him from working his butt off to accomplish his dreams. Yeah, he had to work two jobs, go to night school, and function without sleep, but they'd made it. They had a beautiful house in Edenbury, Pennsylvania, two stylish vehicles in the driveway, and their daughter was heading off to Harvard.

As soon as he finalized the contract he'd been working on for the last year, Wade could take Vanessa on as many getaways as she wanted. He'd cashed the first check on his way home. Just the first installment was more than they'd made their first ten years of marriage. That'd get her eyes twinkling again.

Burnt meatloaf singed his nostrils as he ventured into the kitchen in search of his wife. She'd killed their dinner again. His wife would get so busy typing that she'd forget everything around her.

He turned off the oven, but left the charcoaled mess inside. Last thing he needed was the new smoke detector he'd installed to go off, once again alerting the neighbors how often his wife nearly burnt down their house.

Wade emptied his pockets of his money clip, keys,

and receipts onto the credenza by the stairway, as his wife had always requested, then started upstairs. "Vanessa honey," he called as he trudged up the wooden steps, knowing she wouldn't hear him, but he tried anyway. He gripped the banister, pulling himself forward. He was too tired to climb stairs before eating. But since she always wore her headphones when she worked, she wouldn't hear if he screamed at the top of his range.

Tugging at his tie, he pushed open their bedroom door. Maybe they could have a quick romp before dinner, get a taste of what it'll be like to be empty nesters.

Not believing his eyes, he launched headfirst toward his wife. "No!" he screamed.

Out of his peripherals, he saw a long black rod, but it was too late to react. The little bit of light in the room extinguished the moment the object made contact with his skull, leaving him in a pit of blackness, a nightmare he'd never escape.

CHAPTER 1

Detective Mark Waters smacked the phone onto his desk after he hit *send*. He'd added a heart and smiley face, but he knew Ashlyn saw through him. He wasn't happy that she'd gone to stay with her mother. Especially since she and her mother didn't even get along.

But what could he say? He wasn't her husband. He wasn't even her unborn child's father. He wanted to be, though. He'd asked Ashlyn to marry him last week, and although she'd accepted his ring, she'd run off to her mother as soon as she'd gotten the time off work approved.

He understood she felt guilty that she was pregnant ... blamed herself for the father's death. But he'd told her a hundred times she was innocent, and that he didn't care that she was carrying another man's child. Plain and simple, he loved her. He didn't care about anything else. But for some reason, he couldn't seem to convince Ashlyn.

Mark took a pull off the stuff the station called coffee, nearly gagging. He'd skipped picking up his normal brew in his urgency to pick up Ashlyn and take her to the train station. The last thing he wanted was her second-guessing how he felt about her, even though he was wondering if she returned his sentiment.

"Waters!" Captain Andrew Davis shouted before he even entered the detective's division. Davis had such a booming voice he could have called from his office on the other side of the police station and Mark would have heard him.

Knowing how Davis demanded respect, Mark stood to greet him. "Yeah, Cap'n?"

"You got a stiff."

Mark narrowed his eyes in confusion, wondering why Davis was delivering the report, not dispatch. But instead of questioning his superior, he waited for him to finish.

Captain ran his hand over his chin. "We're going

together. My wife called me. Said she found the body as she was opening for the day."

"I'm sorry," Mark said, knowing Mrs. Davis was probably freaking out about now. The older woman had always held a special place in his heart because of all the years he'd spent in the library when he was a child.

Mark grabbed his radio and keys off his desk, then knocked on the partition surrounding Tim Townsend's cubicle. His partner seemed oblivious that the captain was even in the office, but then again, Townsend was oblivious of most things. Well, except women. If a beautiful woman had walked in, he'd have been on his feet in seconds.

"Let's go, Townsend," Mark demanded, awakening his partner from his comatose-like state that he'd been in for the last week. Even when he was here, he was rarely present.

Townsend dropped his newspaper, looking around as if he hadn't realized he was at work. Based on his crumpled shirt and loose tie, and the fact that his wife had kicked him out again, he'd probably slept here. "What's up?"

Mark cocked his head toward the captain, who'd remained by the door. His silence made it clear that

The Library

he had no interest in talking with Townsend. Davis had warned Mark that Townsend was almost through. Townsend used to be a good detective. Saw things no one else saw. Could pull a confession out of a witness or a guilty party. But he'd screwed up his personal life so badly he was barely fit to be a meter maid, as Mark always threatened.

"We got a dead guy at the library," Mark said, then added in a lower voice, "Mrs. Davis found him."

"Ohh ..." Townsend mused in a breath that came out as a whistle. So he had a fraction of his wits left anyway. He obviously understood that the captain would expect him to handle this case swiftly and professionally.

Mrs. Davis loved her job as head librarian, and she loved the library. She wouldn't tolerate anything tarnishing its reputation after she'd worked so diligently to get the landmark listed as a historical monument so the city wouldn't bulldoze it.

Mark followed Captain Davis to the parking area with Townsend trailing behind him. The sound of the middle-aged detective munching on popcorn irritated him. And Mark knew, just as sure as he was walking, that Townsend would want to ride with him so he could spend the time tapping away on his iPhone, which would further grate on him.

Though the man was in his late forties, he spent most of the workday on his phone. Mark had a smart phone too, but he rarely played on it. Too many important things to do. Townsend was addicted to surfing online dating sites — rather, hook-up sites. And when he wasn't there, he'd play *Angry Birds*. Mark wouldn't mind so much if he'd just turn off the volume. But he had to remind Townsend that the non-stop squawking was nerve-racking.

"You drivin'?" Townsend mumbled around a mouthful of popcorn as they approached their unmarked patrol cars. It wasn't Mark's vehicle, of course, but each detective had their own car, which they treated as though it were theirs. And unlike Townsend's vehicle that smelled like day-old coffee and fried food, Mark kept his cruiser free of fast-food bags, and it always smelled fresh.

"Not if you're eating," Mark barked over his shoulder. "It'd take months for that smell to disappear."

"Sheesh, Waters," Townsend grumbled. "Why so cranky this morning?" He snickered. "Had it out with the woman?"

The Library

Mark ignored Townsend, but realized he *was* allowing his personal life to affect his attitude at work. Only twenty-nine and he sounded like an old man even to himself. Of course, having an eight-month-pregnant girlfriend who didn't know what she wanted was enough to drive any man insane.

Ashlyn was wonderful, though. One of the smartest women he'd ever dated. Even pregnant, she'd finished her bachelor's degree and was interning at a publishing house. Her initial thought was that she'd wanted to run a business, but then a friend offered her a summer internship, and she fell in love with the idea of publishing. When the company offered her a full-time position, even while pregnant, she'd decided immediately to start her new career.

His thoughts traveled to their time together this morning. He'd driven her to the train station as she'd requested, but he hadn't wanted to let her go.

He'd heard her mother's snide remarks when they'd visited her during a 4th of July cookout. Without him being there, she'd be free to spew her rubbish. Ashlyn's mother had insisted that she could do so much better than attaching herself to "a cop," as she'd so rudely insinuated.

It didn't matter that Mark had been running his

own online business for years. He'd set up the website for his widowed mother as something to do in her spare time. But the couponing website had become so popular that he'd ended up having to manage it. His mother hunted down all the promotions, and he took care of everything else behind the scenes.

Ashlyn's mother had the ridiculous idea that Ashlyn needed to marry a doctor or lawyer. The scorned woman couldn't imagine that Ashlyn didn't need a man to take care of her, even though she had one who wanted to with everything he had. If only Mark could make her mother see. Though he knew Ashlyn didn't care about her mother's opinion of him, he knew it'd be one less stress on her. He supposed the only way to convince her mother would be to wave his bank statement in front of her face.

Despite the fact that Ashlyn's previous boyfriends had been ultra-wealthy, she insisted that Mark was everything she wanted in a man. As well as Mark did financially, he knew he couldn't compete with their ultra-wealth.

At least Ashlyn had always told him how much she loved that he kept in shape but didn't have the physique of a bodybuilder, just tall and lean. And she'd always commented on his green eyes and insisted on

The Library

running her hands through his dark hair, which he'd let grow out a little for her benefit. He still kept it short enough that the cowlicks didn't get out of control, though. She loved his curls; he, of course, hated them, as most guys did.

And they enjoyed doing everything together, so what else did she want? Why would a woman say you were everything she'd ever wanted, but then run to her mother days later? A mother she didn't even get along with. Granted, she'd accepted his ring, but she refused to discuss a wedding date, insisting she needed to take care of a few loose ends in her past first.

Forcing his attention back to his job, Mark parallel parked behind the captain's police-issued Crown Vic. His eyes darted to the nineteenth-century structure you'd expect to see on the French countryside, not a Pennsylvania city founded on coal mining. He had an affinity for old buildings, but not as much as he used to after his last experience inside an old train station turned restaurant, something he and Ashlyn had promised never to speak of again.

He exited the cruiser and glanced up at the edifice with its high slanted roof and dormer gables straight out of the Renaissance era. No gaudy colors, just soft gray limestone and medina stone. The old building emanated stateliness. The decorative trim over every door and window beckoned passersby to come in and discover its mysteries.

Pushing through the black-iron gate, Mark smiled as he remembered coming here when he was a young boy. Every Saturday morning, Mrs. Davis would gather the students around a massive marble fireplace for story time. But before she'd start reading, she'd pass the book around to the students. Each child had to inhale the pages, thereby infusing the scent and memory as one into their subconscious.

Mark recalled the scent as having the same rustic aroma of an oak tree after it had fallen in the woods, reminding him of the couple of times he'd sat next to his father while he'd hunted. When the breeze had blown just right, a sweet, pungent smell of the rotting wood wafted into the tree stand.

As a boy, he'd thought the old books were slowly rotting away too, and now the two memories would forever share space in his heart and soul. He also distinctively remembered a delicate hint of jasmine. Then again, he'd sat so close to Mrs. Davis, anxious to receive every word, that it could have been her.

He'd recognized the scent since his mother had planted jasmine in their backyard. The rambling vine

The Library

had spread across the patio and up the fence, filling his summer days with a memorable scent that would forever remind him of his mother and father sipping tea on the back porch before dinner.

Mark ran his hands down the smooth worn wood that framed the door as he entered the library, reveling in the intricate craftsmanship and design.

As soon as he stepped over the threshold, though, his phone buzzed. He glanced at the screen then shot a questioning look over his shoulder at Davis, holding his phone up as a request before answering the call. "Ashlyn's traveling, and I'm a little worried. Do you mind?"

Davis waved him off. "Nah. Go ahead. The old man's dead. He ain't going anywhere."

Mark cocked his head at Davis' apathetic comment, but said, "Thanks" and clicked *answer*, strolling toward the walkway adjacent the library. "Hey, babe! Your mom picked you up already?"

"Not yet," she said, her voice attempting to compete with the racket in the background.

Mark plugged his right ear so he could hear. "She on her way?"

"Yeah," she said. "She texted me a couple seconds ago, saying she'd be here in a few minutes."

He grumbled a half-hearted, "Great," his blood boiling at her mother's lack of concern for anyone other than herself. What woman leaves her eight-month-pregnant daughter waiting at a train station? He knew he should have talked her out of going.

"Mark," she broke him out of his thoughts. "Hang on. Let me get to a quieter place." He heard her labored breaths, and then the noise seemed to lessen as if someone had turned off the volume with a twist of a knob. "I'm fine," she finally said, and he could hear the echo. She must have gone in the washroom. "You really need to stop worrying about me. Okay?"

"That's not going to happen anytime soon, Ash. It's what I do."

She laughed. "I know. Your mother warned me, said you've been worried about her since you were ten."

"Well, I was the man of the house. It's what was expected."

"I'm fine. I just need to clear my head," she said, touching on the subject she obviously knew really worried him.

They'd been dating for six months, and everything seemed to be going well. Just the last month had been rough. He'd stop by her house and find her crying. When he asked, her answer was always, "nothing."

The Library

He'd done some research and chalked it up to hormones until she'd suggested spending the last month of her pregnancy with her mother. Her announcement had floored him. She and her mother fought like cats and dogs. Nothing Ashlyn ever did was good enough for her mother.

"I understand …" he answered her, doing his best not to sound whiny. He hated guys who whined. Though really, he didn't understand, since everything seemed to go sour after he'd proposed. He thought it was what she wanted. They'd spoken of marriage several times in the last few months. It shouldn't have blindsided her, but apparently, she wanted to take care of issues created by her ex before she committed to a date. Whereas Mark thought it'd be good to be married before the baby was born. "I just wish you were —"

"Hey, babe," Ashlyn cut in, "Mom just texted me that she's pulling in, so I should go. I'll call you tonight before I go to bed, okay?"

He gulped down his despair, wanting to give her all the space she needed, but also wanting to understand what more she wanted. "Sure. Love you. Oh, and, Ash … make sure she's not texting while driving."

"Okay, worrywart." She laughed. "And I love you

too, so stop worrying," she replied, and then the line went quiet.

Mark closed his eyes and inhaled a deep breath, attempting to calm himself before going inside to do his job. The sweet scent of jasmine hit him, and he inhaled again, turning to look for the source. He hadn't seen the familiar vine around the entrance, and he didn't suspect that he could smell Mrs. Davis from outside unless she'd suddenly started dousing herself in all sorts of jasmine products.

"Are you the detective?" A soft voice at his six startled him. Rarely was someone able to sneak up behind him.

Mark whipped around to see a stunning redhead at the end of the stone walkway. She was leaning against the wall as if she'd been standing there all morning, just waiting until he finished his phone call.

He thought back to his conversation, wondering if he should be embarrassed about anything he'd said. "Um ... yeah. Mark Waters." He always gave his entire name, which usually prompted the other person to do the same. "And you are ..." He left his words dangling, hoping she'd fill in the blank.

"Jay. I volunteer here."

He should have guessed she was a librarian by the

button-to-the-top white blouse and black skirt, her scarlet hair clipped high on top of her head. The only thing that was missing was the glasses. But based on her age — he guessed her to be about twenty-two — she probably didn't need them yet.

Not knowing where the man had died, he gestured to the front door. "Did you know the deceased?"

She nodded, then released a soft groan. "He was the sweetest old man. We started playing chess about six months ago, but sometimes I'd just listen as he talked about his family. Why would they kill him?"

"That was going to be my next question." He took a step toward her, thinking she was a good person to start his investigation with, but in response, she stepped away. He stopped his forward momentum and instead mirrored her pose, crossing his arms over his chest. "You said 'they' ... Who're 'they'?"

Jay shrugged. "Whoever did this."

"What was the man's name?"

"His friends called him Buck."

"Friends?" Mark uncrossed his arms and sat on the edge of the brick wall, hoping she'd loosen up a bit. Normally when he crossed his arms in reaction to a witness's pose, then uncrossed them, they'd follow suit. Jay remained where she was, however, her arms folded over her chest to protect her from anyone getting too close. If she were sitting, she'd have her legs crossed too, he suspected. "Did Buck belong to a book club?"

She bit down on her lip, her head lowering in her distress. "No. Buck was homeless. We have many homeless people who loiter around the library, especially as the temperature starts to drop. They stay as late as possible, then usually find a place to sleep for the night, and then are here waiting for us to unlock the doors in the morning."

"Did you find him?" he asked, even though Davis had said his wife found the man.

"No. Mrs. Davis found him."

"Do you remember anyone ever arguing with him?" He rephrased the question she'd answered before he'd asked her. Maybe she didn't think someone would have wanted to kill the man, but maybe she'd seen something she'd forgotten.

She shrugged. "Not really. Only the normal stuff. Homeless people tend to ramble on to no one in particular, so most people don't pay them any mind. As long as they're not tarnishing their area. Then there are others like Buck. Buck was a good man; he didn't belong here."

The Library

Mark nodded, noticing the woman had a soft spot for the homeless community, evidently from the time spent with them. He reached in his pocket and pulled out a business card, offering it to her. "Here's my number. Call me —"

The young woman refused the card, shaking her head. "I know how to find you. I don't have any pockets, so I'd just lose it."

He couldn't help but smile at her remark, and though she struggled, her lips edged up for an instant, then fell again. Her amber-colored eyes filled with sorrow. Sad. She was beautiful. And too young to experience this kind of hurt, but he saw it all the time.

Her skin was a creamy ivory color with a flush of pink across her cheeks that counteracted the grief in her eyes. The young woman had a Gaelic look to her as Ashlyn did, except that she was shorter, more soft-spoken. And instead of Ashlyn's strawberry-blond hair, Jay had fiery red hair, a deep crimson shade that looked as if it might burst into flames at any moment.

Not that he was interested. He loved Ashlyn. But he still recognized a beautiful woman when he saw one. And even if Ashlyn ended their relationship tomorrow, he wouldn't date a younger woman.

At twenty-three, Ashlyn was only six years younger

than he was, but it was the furthest he was going. If Ashlyn were even a couple years older, she probably wouldn't be thinking so much about setting a wedding date. They were a perfect couple. They enjoyed each other's company, liked the same things, had similar goals and dreams. Or maybe Mark just thought they wanted the same things in life.

He turned his attention back to the woman in front of him, instead of the one who was hours away. "Can I get your phone number, then, in case I have a question?"

"I live in a dorm and I don't have a phone." She pushed herself away from the wall and walked toward the entrance. "As I said, I know how to find you."

"Okay." Mark knew better than to press a potential witness in public. Unless she was a suspect — and he had evidence to prove she was a suspect — all he could do was hope that she'd cooperate. Behind closed doors, on the other hand, he'd get them to break, find out what they were hiding. Even if they weren't guilty, witnesses tended to get scared, especially when it came to a murder investigation.

He watched for a couple of seconds as the young woman walked toward the entrance, and then turning away, lifted his phone to text Ashlyn. He just wanted

The Library

to make sure she wasn't sitting in the train station. Train stations were some of the scariest places for a single young woman to be alone. But being so far along in her pregnancy, she hadn't wanted to take even the short flight to her mother's house. At least it was better than a bus.

Ashlyn texted him back immediately: *In the car with Mom. Love you, worrywart. ? <3*

He sent back a smiley face and heart in response and made his way to the front door again.

"'Bout time," Captain called, gesturing to the back doors. "Forensics is on the way. Everything good with Ash?"

"Yeah, she's spending a few weeks with her mother before the baby comes," Mark said as nonchalantly as he could muster, but Davis and Townsend raised their eyebrows in unison. A shadow of a smile crossed Townsend's face, but Davis at least had the decency to look concerned.

It wasn't as though Townsend and Mark hung out. The middle-aged man just liked to hear stories, and men in relationships didn't talk about their women the way single men did. When a man loves a woman, he doesn't share sweet or juicy details. The last thing a man wants is for another man to think about his woman in that way. Not that men wouldn't anyway. He couldn't imagine there was a man alive who would look at Ashlyn and not instantly fantasize about her.

With her long legs, perfectly proportioned curves, and flowing strawberry-blond hair, she was a walking pin-up girl. The kind of woman magazines hired to advertise crotch rockets and muscle cars. Not pregnant of course, but he hadn't seen any fewer heads turn after she started showing. If anything, he swore she got more attention.

Mark shot a glance around the library for Jay, but she must have gone straight to work. Oh well, she didn't sound as if she was ready to talk even if she did know something. He'd give her a couple of days and then show up unannounced. Mark followed the group out the rear doors to the patio area.

Although bits of mortar were yellowish and crumbling, the vine-covered brick wall surrounding the area stood tall and sturdy. And he found the source of the jasmine. For a moment, he'd wondered if it had been Jay's perfume.

Only one exit existed on the far-right side of the courtyard. The shiny black-iron gate appeared to have recently received a fresh coat of spray paint and looked solid, so they must have left it unlocked.

He quickened his pace to catch up with Mrs. Davis. When he placed his hand on her forearm, she jumped. But the moment she made eye contact with him, she looked as though she wanted to collapse in his arms. Her eyes were bloodshot, but a gentle smile creased the corners of her lips and eyes.

"Markey," she said through a sigh, giving him a sideways hug. "I don't see enough of you, young man."

He smiled at the woman and her sweet nickname for him. Few people called a six-four cop "Markey" and got away with it, but she always would. He'd never understood why a woman like Margaret Davis had married Captain Davis. She was so mild mannered, and Davis had all the gentleness of a bull. Though, not around her. When Davis was with his wife, he was a different man, as though her kindness slew the wild beast.

"I know, Mrs. Davis. I just can't seem to fit story time into my schedule. I miss it though." He inhaled deeply, thankful the cool September morning had preserved the dead guy enough that he hadn't begun to smell yet.

Her smile grew. "I told you that you'd never forget. It's calming, isn't it?"

"It is," Mark agreed. "The scent takes me back. I can

almost hear you reading *James and the Giant Peach*. I think I was seven at the time, but I can still recall the voices you used for each insect."

Obviously remembering why he was here, Mrs. Davis leaned against him as they approached the homeless man.

Mark focused his eyes on the closed gate again, then scanned the rest of the patio. "Is the gate locked?"

"Yes. We usually open it in the morning and then lock it before we leave. That's what I was coming out to do when I saw him."

"But it was locked when you got here?"

Covering her mouth, she nodded her answer.

"And according to your husband, there's a security system attached to all the doors and windows, but not the patio gate, right?"

"Yes," she choked out.

"Is it possible someone locked two people out here, they fought, and then one slipped by you this morning?"

Mrs. Davis quickly moved her head back and forth. "I checked, Markey. I locked up last night, and I opened this morning. I may seem old, since you were a child when I read to you, but I'm only fifty-three, young man." She tapped her temple. "And my mind is as sharp as it was when I was twenty-three. No one was on the patio either time."

Mark inspected the walls again. Ten feet, he'd guess. Some people could scale them, but ... Mark scrutinized the man on the ground. He appeared to be in his seventies. Long tattered overcoat, shabby work boots. His hands were tanned dark with years of dirt embedded under his fingernails. But there were no scratches on his hands from the vine, no dust from the crumbling brick.

He couldn't envision this seventy-year-old homeless guy climbing the wall. Why would he? The patio held nothing special, no salvation from the elements, no fire pit to keep warm.

The brick-lined courtyard just had a few picnic tables and shrubbery. Marble chess pieces sat on a painted chessboard atop one of the concrete tables. That must have been where Jay and the old man had played chess.

How could someone have murdered the man inside the enclosure and then disappeared? More than likely, Mrs. Davis had been mistaken about locking someone out here, but Mark would never challenge her assertion.

CHAPTER 2

Jay went to the patio as she did every night after everyone else left, but she wouldn't be playing chess with Buck anymore. The thought choked her up more than all the other secrets she'd carried. Instead of leaving though, she huddled in a corner of the courtyard and waited. Not sure what she'd hear or what she could do, but somehow, she needed to end all the secrets forever.

Her only friend other than Buck had told her that Detective Mark Waters was the key. If he could find out what happened, he could fix everything, she was sure. She just wasn't certain how to go about telling him what she'd found.

The familiar creak of the gate opening made her

smile. The maintenance men hadn't thought to fix the eerie squeal when they'd given the iron a new coat of paint. If anything, it stuck even more, sending a shrill through the area.

Since the weather was still nice in September, the homeless community liked coming here. They enjoyed the minimal privacy of being able to talk amongst each other without business owners shooing them away for loitering.

Buck had always kept everyone in line, made sure they were all gone before the sun came up. And then, when the nights turned colder, his band of misfits, as he called them, would head out to an abandoned mill Buck had found for them.

Buck didn't belong here, but he'd made the degenerates of society — the people no one else wanted — his family. She was happy to sit back and watch the mismatched group interact, and she'd always get one game of chess out of the old man before he fell asleep.

Murmurs echoed within the bricked-in area, but Jay remained hidden in her spot. She knew what they were discussing, knew they wanted justice, but also knew they wouldn't get it. Only one person had any knowledge of who killed Buck, but unfortunately, that person was dead.

CHAPTER 3

Mark rolled into the police station's parking area, but didn't get out of his vehicle. He'd sent Ashlyn a text at the last stoplight, and she answered him, but then he'd caught every green light on the way to work. Aggravating how when you want a red light, you get all green lights. If he were running lights and siren on the other hand, every one of the five lights on his route into work would have been bright red.

In the privacy of his car, he huffed out a breath at their discussion. Once he got inside the department, he couldn't reveal any more of his personal life than he already had. They should be having this conversation in person ... or at least over the phone. But since her mother was hovering over her, she didn't want to talk where she could hear.

Screw it, he thought. He touched her name on his *favorites* screen.

"Mark ..." she complained as soon as she answered.

"Go outside, please. Our conversation is none of your mother's business. And I know she thinks it's none of mine, but she's wrong." He inhaled a deep breath before he said his next words, the words he'd been contemplating all night. "Unless I'm wrong. If we're over, if you've decided to turn down my marriage proposal and break it off completely, then I guess this isn't my business."

"Hang on," she said on a long drawn-out breath.

He wasn't sure if it was because she was aggravated with him or because she was tired from the trip. It couldn't be easy traveling all day when you're that far along. Her mother muttered something, but it sounded muffled, so Ashlyn must have cupped the phone.

"Okay." She let out another extended breath. "Let me just get to the bench. It's tiring walking and talking."

"I'm sorry, baby," he offered. "I'm not trying to give you a hard time. I'm just —"

"I know, Mark," she cut in. "And, no, I don't want to break up. I can't believe you asked me that." She pulled in a deep breath and then a small whimper escaped he was sure she hadn't wanted him to hear.

"Oh, Ashlyn, please don't cry. God, I hate to hear you cry. I just want to talk about this, and I hate that you're not here."

"I'm not crying because of you. I know you only want what's best. Mom thinks — insists — that I tell them. That it's the right thing to do."

Mark pinched the bridge of his nose. It *was* the right thing to do — *is* the right thing — and he knew it. He just didn't want her to do it, and her mother couldn't care less if it was the right thing to do. She just wanted the notoriety she thought it'd bring, not caring how the situation would affect Ashlyn and her unborn child.

"It is the right thing to do, Ash. I've told you I think it is. But I care about what's right for you, not them. They'll fight you for custody, you know. Right after they demand blood tests and insist the department reopen the case, they'll fight for custody of their only grandchild."

This time she couldn't mask her tears. A burst came

out as she tried to speak. "I ... know ... that's why I'm so scared."

Feeling eyes on him, Mark surveyed the parking lot while he let Ashlyn pour out the tears she needed to expel. No one was in the vicinity, but he saw Townsend's old Trans-Am — another one of his midlife-crisis purchases — so it probably had been him. Strange that he hadn't heard it, though. Townsend had souped up the engine by adding mufflers, headers, and a plethora of other aftermarket accessories Mark had no understanding of or desire to know about. He simply took his truck to get an oil change, rotated the tires, and did whatever else the manual called for as routine service.

He returned his attention to Ashlyn, waiting for her crying to subside before he spoke. "Then why are you there?" He took in a breath to soften his words and quickly continued, "I'm sorry. That's not what I meant to say. I don't have a problem with you visiting your mother. You know I want you and her to get along. But for you to bring up talking to them while you're away ... I just don't understand. We should be discussing this together ... here."

"It's just not right that I keep unloading all my troubles on you, Mark. My pregnancy happened before we met, so it's only fair that I take care of the issue."

Though she obviously couldn't see him, he rolled his eyes at her comment. Well, especially because she couldn't see him. He wouldn't act so childish in front of her, but how ridiculously childishly was she behaving. They'd had this conversation over and over. "Ashlyn, I asked you to marry me. I set up everything to give you the fairy-tale proposal you deserve. I did it because I love you, all of you, even your problems. Whether your problems are in your past, present, or future, I want your troubles to be my troubles, your heartaches to be my heartaches, and your victories to be my victories. And I want to be the father of your child. Why can't you understand that?"

"I know you do, Mark. And it was a beautiful proposal. Never in my life had I imagined such a wonderful day. The Poconos were breathtaking, the horse-drawn carriage magical, and the ring ... Why did you buy such a gorgeous ring? I never wanted anything that extravagant —"

"'Never wanted anything that extravagant,'" Mark jumped on her words, "meaning you wanted it." He hated that his words sounded desperate, but he loved her and refused to let any opportunity slip away. If he had to use his detective skills to read between the lines, so be it. Because the thought that she could doubt for a second whether they should spend the rest of their lives together had knocked him in the gut. He couldn't see himself with anyone but Ashlyn ever again.

"Of course I want to marry you, dreamed of you proposing. I said yes, accepted your ring. I just realized I had to figure out what to do in my situation before we set a date though. We've been so busy these last six months that I've ignored reality. And the reality is that he's their grandson, their only grandson. And even if Devin was a putz, a murderer even, his child is still their grandson."

Mark exhaled a breath of relief. "Thank you. It just scared me that you ran off. But I understand you need to do what's best for both of you. I just wish I could be there when you talk to him, but you know I can't. Devin's father would recognize me. Just don't do anything without thinking this through, please."

"I won't. I'll take a couple of days and think about it before I do anything rash."

"Sorry for worrying so much. I love you, so I care."

"I know you do. I love you too. I'll talk to you later, okay?"

The Library

"Yeah. I have to go to work. Got a murder case to solve, ya know?"

"Good luck. It has to be easier than my case," she said, a nervous chuckle seeping through her words.

"Let's hope!"

Mark clicked *end*, closed his eyes, and leaned against the leather headrest. He knew Ashlyn should tell them; he just didn't want her to get hurt. After speaking with Devin Burke's father when he wanted answers about his son's death and hearing about the man's ruthless business tactics, he anticipated Gregory Burke would cause Ashlyn plenty of trouble. Especially when he found out that Ashlyn's new boyfriend just so happened to be the investigating officer of his son's death. Not good. Not good at all.

Mark had told Captain Davis what he discovered, even showed him the evidence. Davis had agreed; Devin's case had been a suicide by train.

But Mr. Burke would insist that the captain reopen the case, would drag Ashlyn through a court battle she couldn't afford, and generally just make their lives a nightmare. Yes, telling the Burkes about their grandson was the right thing to do. But what was the right thing for Ashlyn and her unborn son?

He'd be willing to bet Ashlyn's mother couldn't care

less about doing the right thing. Her only concern was that Ashlyn's son was the only living heir to one of the wealthiest and most powerful families in Pennsylvania.

CHAPTER 4

Mark made his slow way into the station, taking the civilians' corridor to the visitors' area coffee station, instead of the employees' lounge. Not that it mattered. Tim would pummel him for information in their office just as much as he would in the break room. The difference was that Mark would have a distraction behind his computer, and Tim wouldn't have an audience.

After pouring soot-colored muck into his chrome mug — since he hadn't had time to make his normal stop for drinkable coffee again — he headed down the back corridor. He'd bypass the employees' lounge, but he'd have to walk past the captain's office. More than likely he wouldn't have made it into work yet, though.

A woman's sobbing caught his attention, and he slowed his gait.

"Mark," Captain Davis called, gesturing him inside.

Mark stepped inside the lavishly furnished space, as opposed to his six-by-six cubicle, and put a hand on Mrs. Davis' shoulder. "You okay?" He sat down in the leather chair beside her.

Captain Davis pulled out a handkerchief and handed it to his wife. "Honey, no one is sabotaging the library. It was probably just a bunch of kids."

The older woman shook her head. "But how did they get inside? I double checked every window and door after what happened yesterday." She dropped her head. "I thought since the library was in the historical register that it would be the end of the greedy developers, but I guess it can have uses for something other than a library and still fit their plans of commercializing the area into a massive outdoor mall. As though we need another shopping center."

Davis shook his head. "Honey, do you honestly think someone would murder a man in order to close the library? That's a little drastic."

Her head snapped up at her husband's remark. "Yes, I do. When it comes to money, I wouldn't put anything past those greedy developers, especially since most of them look at the homeless community as worthless anyway." Her eyes darted to Mark. "What have you found? Do you know who murdered that poor old man?"

Surprised at her sudden shift to him, Mark quickly shook his head. "Um, no, ma'am. Not yet, but I'll do my best."

Captain Davis stood and walked around his desk. "Mark, I want you to follow Margaret and check out the scene." Davis knelt down in front of his wife. "Mark is the best we have, honey. He'll figure out what's going on. I promise." Davis glanced up at Mark, assuring him that he'd better prove him right.

Per the captain's orders, Mark drove Mrs. Davis to the library in her vehicle. Davis had assured him that he'd send Townsend to pick him up as soon as he was finished going over the area.

Since nothing was missing, and no one had been murdered — inside — Mrs. Davis begged Mark not to tear apart her library looking for evidence and fingerprints. But to just do his best.

Typical, Mark thought, *find the bad guy, but don't interfere with my life*. Again, he'd kept his comments to himself, especially since he had all the respect for the woman who'd spent most of her life serving the public.

As soon as they stepped inside, Mrs. Davis escorted Mark to the reference area of the enormous building. Jay stood at the railing of the second floor, her blazing-red hair causing her to stand out like a beacon even inside the shadowy building. Her intense glower as she spoke to a vagrant indicated that she was upset about something. The man didn't as much as offer a nod in response; he just stared blankly at the books on the shelves. No doubt the man was homeless based on his ragged overcoat and shabby appearance. He was cleaner than most, though, so he must be newly down on his luck.

Mark studied the man's face, committing it to memory. More than likely Jay recognized the man as one of Buck's friends and wanted to question him. Civilians always wanted to do the detective's job. He'd have to find out what she knew or thought she knew.

Retracting her eyes from the man for a brief second, Jay glanced downward and offered Mark a soft smile and a friendly wave as he passed beneath her.

Mark waved back, hoping he hadn't conveyed interest in her yesterday. She hadn't seemed attracted to him, but now she was smiling and waving. *Stupid man*, Mark thought, *she's just being nice*. Just because a young woman smiles at you, doesn't mean she's interested.

The problem was he tended to be too nice. He had a hard time telling people no, especially women. Already, Ashlyn was jealous because he'd helped Anna, a woman in forensics, put in a water heater. Anna was beautiful, no doubt, but Ashlyn had no reason to be jealous. He had no desire for any woman but Ashlyn. But he'd made the mistake of telling Ashlyn he had a fondness for redheads, especially strawberry blondes, thinking Ashlyn would realize he was talking about her, not other women. But Anna had strawberry-blond hair too, and he had to work with her, which had made Ashlyn question if he was attracted to her. Mark could have slapped himself for telling Ashlyn about his affair with the police dispatcher. Pregnant women, he realized, tended to get jealous easily.

"Only signs of vandalism are in here," Mrs. Davis said, pulling him from his personal thoughts. She gestured around the windowless room strewn with papers, folders, and books of every size, shape, and color. "I'm sure they were looking for something from zoning, anything to find a reason to shut us down."

Mark nodded, even though he felt the same as

Captain Davis. Why would anyone think trashing a place would cause the city to close the library? And he couldn't imagine that some land developer would go so far as murdering someone because they wanted a piece of commercial property.

Mark pointed to a filing cabinet with rows and rows of boxes about three inches wide. The drawer stood open, but it didn't look as though anything had been disturbed. "What's that?" he asked as he approached the beige seven-drawer cabinet.

Mrs. Davis walked up beside him. "It *has* been a while, Markey. You've never used microfilm?"

He shook his head. "Nope. Google all the way."

She closed the drawer. "Well, they didn't mess with those, thank goodness. That would have been a mess." Mrs. Davis squeezed his arm. "Please find out who did this. I don't want to be afraid to come to the place that has always been my sanctuary."

"I'm sorry, Mrs. Davis. I promise I'll do my best."

She patted his arm and walked off.

Mark's eyes raked over the room. Where the heck would he start?

Not that it mattered, since she'd put her hands everywhere, and hundreds of other hands had been here before him, but he pulled on his latex gloves and

The Library

went to work. He decided to start from one wall and work his way across the entire room, looking for anything the thief might have been searching for, checking to see if anything had been torn or removed from any of the books. More than likely, the destruction was a cover-up.

Every shelf had been cleared in the fifty-by-fifty space. He spent hours sifting through encyclopedias, medical reference books, and dictionaries, wondering why they still kept the relics. The information was so outdated it couldn't possibly be of any use.

Three hours later, Mark came full circle to the only thing in the room that hadn't been touched. The cabinet filled with microfilm. If kids did this, or someone who just wanted to cause a mess for them to clean up, why not scatter this information too?

He pulled out the drawer and ran his finger down the row of white boxes housing the microfilm. He picked up a few and read off the contents. Old newspapers dating back to the early 1900s.

"Did you find something?" The same soft voice from yesterday, coupled with the familiar hint of jasmine, penetrated his contemplations.

Mark turned and leaned against the cabinet. "Not yet. Just so happens to be the only thing not touched."

He held up the white box he'd been reading. "Do you know how to use these?"

"No, but Mrs. Davis does. I keep to the fiction. I always was a sucker for epic novels, the stories where the heroine beats the odds, masters the game of life, and then lives happily ever after. Too bad that rarely happens."

Not sure how to interpret her comment, he simply nodded in response and moved toward questioning her again, "Did you think of anything else?"

"No, but I'll let you know if I do." Jay walked off, silencing his attempt at digging deeper as she'd done yesterday. He'd give her another day at most, but then he'd push her to come down to the station. He couldn't force her, of course. Unless someone agrees to take the witness stand in court, everyone has the right to remain silent. Mark loved how TV shows always showed a detective dragging a suspect or witness in for questioning. He could ask all the questions he wanted, but ... suspect or witness, it didn't matter; they didn't have to breathe a word.

At least it appeared that Jay hadn't been flirting with him. He'd hate to be rude. Mark shoved the container back in its spot and closed the cabinet. He had to agree with the captain — kids.

The Library

As he headed for the door, the lights flickered behind him. He turned to see the drawer standing open again. Walking toward it guardedly, as if it were a snake, he gulped and peered at the tracking, testing the drawer's weight. It didn't slide easily and was actually rather heavy. He didn't like things opening on their own, though. He pushed the drawer back in and checked the catch. It held firmly.

He walked toward the door again, and the lights flickered a second time. "Oh, God. No ..." he mumbled. Swallowing a mouthful of air, he turned back to the cabinet. He about dropped to his knees when it opened in front of his eyes. "What the hell? Am I a Ghost Buster now?"

Mark stormed toward the cabinet, shoving his hands against the drawer, but it didn't budge. "I'm not doing this again," he said through his teeth. "I need facts. Hard facts. I can't go to my boss with the excuse that a ghost did it." The drawer slammed closed beneath his hands and then popped open, mocking him.

His anger mounting, Mark pulled his fist to his mouth and bit down on his hand to keep from screaming. How was it possible? He didn't believe in ghosts; rather, he didn't want to believe in ghosts.

After The Depot and his friend Gino's experience at The Pit Stop, however, he wasn't sure what to believe.

He threw up his hands. "Fine! I take it I'm supposed to go through every one of these. You realize that will take forever, right? Could you be a sport and point out which one you want me to search?"

"*Markey?*" Mrs. Davis' tone held all the concern it should have. "Do you need me to find something for you?"

He reeled and faced her, forcing a wide grin on his face that he hoped masked the terror in his chest. "Hi, Mrs. Davis. Don't worry about me. It's what detectives do. We ask questions."

She smiled sweetly, but added a nervous chuckle. "Oh. I understand. I talk to myself all the time. Though, I don't usually ask myself to do anything."

He laughed. "Yeah, well, I just realized I need to go through some of these old boxes of microfilm and wasn't sure where to start."

"Really?" she asked, stepping closer, evidently confident that he was the same old Markey and hadn't turned loony on her. "What could you possibly find from old newspapers? I doubt there's anything interesting. I don't even know why we keep them. No one ever looks at them anymore. I even got rid of all but one machine."

Mark shrugged and gazed up at the ceiling as if the ghost would be hovering over him, waiting to provide the answer. "Well, it's the only thing in the room that hasn't been touched. So I thought, what if someone was trying to tell us where to look by knocking everything else out of the way?"

"Clever." Mrs. Davis grinned, wiggling her eyebrows. "I always loved a good mystery. But it's late. Why don't I set up the scanner and we can go through them tomorrow?"

Mark wasn't sure if that was acceptable or not. He stepped forward and closed the drawer, which closed easily, of course. So, the entity only wanted to show off around him, or a more logical explanation was that he was losing his mind.

He took Mrs. Davis' arm and escorted her out of the reference room, glancing back to make certain that the lights and drawer behaved. Nothing moved. So either he was plain mental or the poltergeist only wanted to speak to him. He wasn't sure which thought made him more uncomfortable.

CHAPTER 5

Ashlyn sat at the breakfast table and gazed at the backyard of her mother's beautiful property. The house was ancient, but it held a special place in her heart. The Victorian house had charm that no modern-day home could possibly imitate. Her ancestors had been in this part of Pennsylvania for so long that the road even bore the family name.

She twisted a strand of her hair, then draped it across her face as she'd done when she was a child.

"Ashlyn," her mother admonished. "How many times —"

Ashlyn jerked her head up at her mother, halting her words in their tracks. "I wasn't chewing on my hair, Mother. I was simply —" She stopped defending herself, another habit she'd been doing her entire life, and stood up with her coffee cup. *Hiding*, Ashlyn thought. She'd been trying to hide behind her curtain of hair. Then — and even now. Why? Why did she still let her mother affect her? She pushed open the patio door. "I'm going for a walk."

"Sweetheart," her mother appealed in her saccharine voice, but Ashlyn slammed the door on her phony endearment. She wasn't her sweetheart; she was barely her daughter. Her mother had dragged her from one beauty pageant to another, always looking for fame and fortune, since she'd missed her chance. She'd given Ashlyn her maiden name, the name she'd chosen to keep when she'd married because she thought she'd be famous.

Her mother had asked Ashlyn if she'd been proud of her for giving her a name that was suitable for a Hollywood star, *Ashlyn Allan*. At sixteen, Ashlyn was finished with her mother traipsing her around and showing her off. One day, Ashlyn just screamed at her, insisting that she would no longer be her mother's Barbie doll. Her mother had lashed back at her that it had been her fault that she'd not made it in Hollywood and that she owed her.

It wasn't Ashlyn's fault. Heck, her mother hadn't

even had her until she was twenty-eight. But she blamed the end of her career on her. Well, she blamed it on Ashlyn's father first, and then she blamed it on her only child.

Ashlyn's father had been forty years her mother's senior when she met him. He'd been a high-level exec at MGM, and her mother had believed that he could make her a superstar, albeit he never promised to do that. In fact, he retired right after they married, thinking his new bride would want to settle down.

Her mother had no intention of settling down according to her aunt who confided the entire sordid affair to Ashlyn when she was old enough to understand it. Her aunt had also let it slip how utterly appalled her mother had been when she realized she was pregnant, but then quickly apologized and backtracked her statement, saying she'd just been upset about a movie role she'd lost.

After that, her aunt said Laura had driven her husband crazy, insisting he find her another starring part. Ashlyn's father died of a heart attack before her first birthday, and unable to get any work in Hollywood, her mother had taken her hefty life insurance payment and moved back to Pennsylvania.

Ashlyn breathed in the brisk fall air as she lingered

along the hedge, her hands gingerly caressing the fluffy blossoms of the buttonbushes bordering her grandmother's property. Her heart filled with contentment as she watched the monarch butterflies searching for nectar from the white fragrant flowers that looked like ping-pong-ball-sized pincushions. She loved to retreat to nature, forgetting all the worries in the world — her world.

Her eyes delighted on the array of gold, orange, and even purplish leaves and blossoms that covered the property. She obviously inherited her love of gardening from her grandmother. Ashlyn had filled a notebook with all her favorite ornamental bushes and flowering trees.

Now that Mark had proposed, she thought she might be able to see her dream of a beautiful home come to fruition — a real home, the type of household where the mother and father sat down at the dinner table with the children. The type of family that genuinely enjoyed staying home on a Saturday morning and working in the backyard together. Love. True love. For their life and one another. Of course, in order to be free of her past, she had to face it first. She refused to live a life of secrets, and she refused to lie to her baby.

Ashlyn reached out and pulled down a long stalk covered with red and gold leaves. She dug through the foliage, looking for the cluster of yellowish pods with brown spots. The shrub rewarded her with several of the sticky and fuzzy fruit that contained the sweet, earthy hazelnuts. Based on the outer leafage, the nuts needed a few more days to ripen, but as her grandmother had shown her, she could just toss them in a box and they'd ripen within a few days.

After a few hours with nature, Ashlyn wandered back to the house, hoping her mother had taken a nap or gone to the store. She opened the back door as quietly as possible and then tiptoed through the parlor, as her grandmother had called the formal area that welcomed guests into her home.

Ashlyn peeked through the diamond-shaped glass in the entry door and thrilled at the fact that her mother had left the house. Good riddance. It'd give Ashlyn time to think.

She hadn't made the long and tedious trip up here to be with her mother; she'd come to Erie to be with her grandmother. Well, her grandmother's home, a place where she had a few good memories of her childhood.

Her grandmother had left her some boxes when she

passed, and she'd never gone through them. She figured this would be as good a time as any. Sifting through the musty attic as she'd done when she was a child, trying on the old outfits and hats would be fun.

Ashlyn climbed the stairs to her grandmother's room inhaling the smell that never went away. No matter how many bowls of potpourri or scented candles her mother spread throughout the house, the old place smelled like her grandmother. Actually, she assumed it smelled like her great, great-grandmother, since it went back that far. She couldn't quite place the scent of the abode. It just smelled of wood and years of cooking, but it always smelled like home. An old outhouse even still sat in the backyard. Although, it was no longer an outhouse. One of her relatives had filled it with dirt in the early part of the century.

Unlike newer homes that had a pull-down staircase to get to the attic, the stairway that led to the third floor — fourth if you counted the basement — was a narrow passage through a doorway at the end of the hallway that led straight up. The attic wasn't really an attic, in the sense that it was just space between the ceiling and the roof; instead, the rectangular room stretched the length of the house with a window on either side. The low A-shaped ceiling above her head held nothing but cobwebs and rafters, so the only light was by way of lamps and light from outside. It was spooky, but a sanctuary at the same time.

Ashlyn dragged the large box with her name scribbled across the top under the half-moon-shaped window. The leaded beveled glass cast an intricate spider-web pattern across her treasure chest of memorabilia, sending a spine-chilling sensation over her skin for no apparent reason. Yeah, she'd lived through a ghostly situation once, but she'd never seen anything supernatural before or after. Even now, she wondered if she hadn't just seen some sort of distortion.

She'd asked her grandmother to leave her several things that she knew her mother wouldn't appreciate, but she wasn't sure what else she'd stuffed inside the cardboard box.

As soon as she opened the top closure, Ashlyn jumped and almost hit her head on the low ceiling as a tiny black spider darted over her hand. She laughed as she willed her heart to slow.

"Get out of here," she said softly, shooing the innocent creature away. She'd never been afraid of spiders. They served a purpose, her grandmother had told her. "Without spiders," Mémé had said, "the world would be over-run with insects, and our food crops would be decimated within months."

Still, Ashlyn carefully ventured back into the box. Regardless of the fact that they were necessary, she didn't want an entire family of arachnids traipsing over her. She'd deal with them, but they needed to keep their distance.

Her grandmother had wrapped every item in the crate in fabric, scraps of material she'd had left over from her sewing, Ashlyn was positive. Her grandmother had made all her curtains and slipcovers for years, even some pajamas Ashlyn still had tucked away in her bureau at home.

Old photo albums and vinyl records filled the box, along with books. Lots and lots of books. Some, she was certain, were first editions worth a fortune. She no longer cared about money as she used to, though. Between Mark's ventures and her new career, they would be quite comfortable, more than comfortable actually. More money just meant more problems. Her mother had plenty of money after her father had died, and it hadn't provided her happiness. Fame was what her mother craved.

Thankfully, Ashlyn had no desire for fame or fortune. She ran her hands over her belly, full of life, wondering if her mother felt the joy that she did with the tiny person growing inside her. Yeah, the father was a moron, but that wasn't the baby's fault. And if Mark still wanted to marry her after she'd run off from him, she'd be stupid not to jump at his proposal. She'd always known that he'd make a great husband, and now she was convinced that he'd be a wonderful father too.

Funny how just being in her grandmother's home could help her understand that all she wanted was a loving husband and a healthy son. She'd make sure next time they talked, he understood that just because she asked for time before they set a date didn't mean she was second-guessing marrying him. She'd just been worried about her unborn child.

She un-wrapped another book at the bottom of the box. The simple blue-pebbled cover with a gilt-stitched title *The Joy of Cooking* across the top greeted her. The spine was missing, exposing the stitched binding. A sticky residue where her grandmother or maybe a further ancestor had tried to hold it together marked the bottom of the antique cookbook.

As carefully as she could, she opened the cover, anxious to see if it was a first edition, and if so, the date it was published. "Oh, wow!" she shrieked. "1931!"

The Library

Even in its current shabby condition it was worth a fortune. Not that she'd sell it, but it'd be great to have a first edition of such a popular book in her office.

Unable to resist, she delicately flipped through the pages, smiling at the illustrations sketched inside. Pots and pans, utensils, and other kitchen accessories embellished the headings of each section. As she skimmed across the segment of soufflés, she smiled at the penciled drawings that resembled her buttonbush blossoms she'd been admiring earlier.

A faded note in the margin beside a recipe for pot roast stopped her meandering. *Our first meal.* The penciled words could have been from her great, great-grandmother who would have been in her forties in the thirties, or her grandmother could have written it in the fifties. But what if Edda had scribbled it?

A shiver swept down Ashlyn's arms at the thought that the woman she'd never met, the woman who'd watched over her somehow, had written this about the man whom she'd thought she would marry.

But then a man nobody knew had murdered her great-grandmother, Edda, in 1934 at the age of nineteen after she'd had a baby. She hadn't been living here; she'd left the baby with her mother while she'd worked in Edenbury. But she certainly came back here. More than likely her mother had just packaged up her few belongings after her death.

Nervous at the thought of delving deeper into the secrets of the past, Ashlyn's hands broke into a sweat, but she persisted, knowing she owed her great-grandmother that much. After all, Ashlyn's ex-boyfriend had tried to murder her, and somehow, she was certain that her great-grandmother's ghost had saved her.

One by one, Ashlyn turned each yellowed page, hoping another clue would present itself. Her heart skipped a beat when she came to the dessert section.

Tucked between the brittle and stained pages was a picture. A black and white image of a man. No name, just a date, 1929. Five years before Edda's murder. Edda would have been fourteen, but her fiancé, the father of her child had been away for a few years, her grandmother had said. Could she be holding the graduation picture of Edda's fiancé, Ashlyn's great-grandfather, a man who may have gotten away with murder?

CHAPTER 6

She watched as the thief once again pawed through the books, ever searching. It'd been years, and she'd thought that the murderer would have forgotten all about her family, but evidently seeing Buck had reopened old wounds, dredged up old secrets. But Buck hadn't known anything.

"What did you do with it, Jessica?" the fiend shouted at the ceiling. As always, she tried to recognize the voice, but voices didn't sound the same here. Each word came through individually as a slow and fading echo, as if the sound had passed through several chambers in a massive cathedral. "I know it's here."

She couldn't help but wonder if she should answer, but that would be too easy. Hiding and taunting had always been more fun. Watching as the paranoia tore at her assailant's sanity had provided a modicum of redemption.

When she'd first arrived here in her current condition, the murderer had come to the library constantly. But since Buck had disappeared, so had any concern for an arrest, she supposed. As years earlier, the coward's face was shielded in some ridiculous ski mask, even though there were no security cameras in the library. She'd spent decades waiting, but had never been able to confirm the murderer's identity. Her only guess was that someone had recognized Buck and had returned to silence him once and for all.

Her anger bubbled to the surface. She'd been content to stay here, but hoped that one day she could leave. She glided to the cabinet that housed the microfilm, the only area the villain had yet to check. It wasn't there; she'd moved it years ago. If only she could remember where she put it, maybe she could get the right person to stumble upon it.

Just for fun, she decided to put on a show. She concentrated on the tiny boxes, hoping they were light enough. One by one, she lifted the paper boxes, allowing them to levitate, then threw them at the murderer.

The weakling took off in response, screaming at the ceiling, "Leave me alone."

She blocked the door the best she could, causing the masked intruder to shiver while passing through her. That was all she could do. Toss around a few light objects, cause someone to look over their shoulder at a sound or a flash of light.

The murderer charged out the door. "Forgive me. I'm sorry."

CHAPTER 7

When Mark arrived at the library the next day, he found Mrs. Davis on the outside bench crying. She'd been crying so loudly that she'd nearly bounded over the back of the bench when he stooped down in front of her.

She threw her hands over her chest. "Oh, Markey! You scared the bejesus out of me."

He resisted smiling, but wondered how he'd startled her, since he hadn't been silent coming through the gate. His police-issued black combat boots were quiet with their thick soles, but still, he'd rushed up the walkway when he saw her crying, praying she hadn't found another dead body. Of course, he didn't know that she hadn't found a body, but he assumed that if she'd stumbled upon another murder, it would have been her first words.

"What happened? Are you okay?" he asked once she caught her breath.

Mrs. Davis pursed her lips to hold back her tears and nodded. "I'm fine. Just upset. They came back."

Mark sat down beside her and she immediately leaned against him, making him realize why she'd chosen Captain Davis as a husband. She was smart and strong, but like Ashlyn, she had a soft side. She must have liked that Captain Davis was tall and strong — and a cop. The same aspects Ashlyn had told him she appreciated.

Ashlyn had confessed that she'd always thought she needed to meet a wealthy man to take care of her financially, as her mother had insisted. But after what happened with her ex-boyfriend, she'd said she realized she was quite capable of taking care of herself financially. What she wanted was someone to take care of the monsters in the world and hold her when she needed to be held.

Mark was happy to do both, but assured her he'd be willing to take care of her financially too if she decided to stay home once the baby was born. That part she'd declined, insisting that she could manage her career and being a mother. Mark had no doubt; Ashlyn would be a great mother.

Once Mrs. Davis' hitched breathing subsided, Mark patted her hand, encouraging her to talk to him. "What happened?"

"Oh, Markey. The same thing. Only this time, they went through the microfilm cabinet." She dropped her head. "I just don't understand how they're getting inside the building."

"Is it possible they're inside before you lock up, and then they take off when you're not looking?" he asked.

Her head bobbed. "I guess anything is possible."

Mark stood up and offered her his arm. She gripped his arm and pulled herself up, allowing him to escort her inside. He stopped just inside the front door and pointed to the security system. "Set the alarm." She did as he requested and then he walked her directly to her office. "Lock your office door. I'm going to have a look around. He may have slipped out already, but he may still be here, and I don't want to spook him into thinking he needs a hostage."

Mrs. Davis nodded and closed the door behind him. He waited for the click and then called Captain Davis on his cell.

"How's it goin', Waters?"

The Library

"Not good, Cap'n. Looks like there was another break-in. I locked your wife inside her office, and I'm going to have a look around, but I need to get a team out here. I know Mrs. Davis doesn't want us scouring the library for evidence, and I think fingerprinting would be a waste of time since there are thousands upon thousands of prints here, so at least we won't have black dust everywhere. But whoever's doing this is looking for something, and I'd like to find it first."

"Margaret will understand," Captain offered. "Do me a favor first, though. I know you said you locked my wife in her office, but I'd like her home. Tell her I said so. I'm on my way. I have a few things I want to check on as well."

"O ... kay, Cap'n." Mark hung up the phone, slightly confused. Why on earth would Davis feel the need to be here? Did he not trust that Mark could handle an investigation on his own?

Mark continued to sweep the area with his eyes, his gun held close to his body in case he saw a threat as he touched Townsend's name on his phone screen. He ignored Townsend's disrespectful "Yeah?" as an answer, knowing it bothered the older man that Mark was his superior. They'd discuss it later, though. They had a job to do.

"Call Roland and get over here," Mark demanded. "There was another break-in at the library and we need to find what they're looking for." Mark hung up without waiting for a response, then knocked on the door marked Administration Only. "Mr. Davis said to escort you to your car, Mrs. Davis."

"But I —" she tried, but he shook his head, no sign of the Mark she'd known for twenty years, only the police officer he was trained to be. The look in her eyes revealed she understood. She grabbed her purse and allowed him to escort her to her car after she deactivated the security system.

Mark watched the front entrance as he waited for Mrs. Davis to drive away. Once he saw out of his peripherals that she was gone, he returned to the library and reset the alarm.

"Okay!" Mark shouted inside the cavernous construction. "It's just you and me, and of course, my entire team will be here in a few minutes. So if you don't want some rookie cop with an itchy trigger finger gunning you down, I suggest you come out now." He waited a few seconds, listening for any sounds of life — or death for that matter. Nothing. "Have it your way." Mark ambled toward the reference room.

As Mrs. Davis had said, the place was worse than

The Library

it had been yesterday. The microfilm cabinet he'd planned to go through today was empty, its contents spread across the entire room. He'd been wrong. Someone hadn't left that particular section for him; they'd just failed to get to it, it seemed.

Not knowing where to start, Mark sat down and waited for Roland and Anna to arrive. Since there wasn't a lot of crime in Edenbury, the forensic team consisted of only two people. Well, there didn't used to be. Most of the city's cases were burglaries, with assaults, thefts, robberies, and auto thefts vying for second place. Rape and murder were practically nonexistent. An attempted murder and actual murder in six months in a town with less than seventy thousand people was too high.

"10-23, Waters," Townsend's voice shrilled over the radio, announcing he was *on-scene*.

"10-4." Mark laughed as he headed toward the entry and deactivated the security code. Ever since he was a rookie, the other officers made sure Mark knew they'd arrived. Pull a gun on a cop once and they never forget it, it seemed.

Townsend happened to be his FTO at the time, so the entire department heard about Mark pulling his gun on his field-training officer in the middle of a search of The Depot at three o'clock in the morning. Oh, well, no one had ever snuck up on him again or played practical jokes as they did with the other officers. Nope. They'd figured him for a loaded gun, cocked and ready to explode. It wasn't true, but he'd let them go ahead and think it. After all, his father had been murdered, and his half-sister was awaiting trial for several offenses, so there was slight merit, he guessed.

Mark opened the front entrance door to Townsend, Roland, and then Anna, who breezed by him smelling like summer honeydew. What the heck was it with all the redheads in his life?

"Hi, Mark," she drawled in her soft southern manner. She'd moved to Pennsylvania about eight months ago, after finishing her degree in Columbia, South Carolina. He'd been interested in her the first couple of months, before he'd met Ashlyn, but he'd never made a move because he'd screwed up royally once before by dating one of the police department's dispatchers.

He'd always been smart enough not to date women he worked with. But they'd hooked up unexpectedly at a party one night, and then it'd been impossible just to walk away. Thankfully, after he'd finally ended the relationship, the dispatcher moved to Florida. They were doomed from the start, as they had nothing in common. So he'd ignored his attraction to Anna and her constant flirting, and thank goodness he had, or he wouldn't have met Ashlyn, and she was better than all the women he'd dated combined.

Mark instructed the uniformed officers who'd arrived on scene to monitor the front and rear exits, then directed Roland and Anna to Mrs. Davis' office while Townsend and he did a thorough search of the building. They took turns blocking exits while the other cleared each section of the enormous building.

After twenty minutes, it was clear that the intruder had already left the premises. So either Mrs. Davis had been wrong and hadn't seen anyone as they made their getaway after she'd locked them in all night, or someone had a key to the building and the code to the alarm. Mark would make sure she changed both today.

Once Mark deemed the building clear, he gestured that the library was all theirs. "I'm not sure what we're looking for, guys, but I'd guess it's in the reference section. Follow me."

Mark led the team to the large room at the end of the building, feeling a chill ripple through him as he stepped over the threshold.

"It looks like a twister touched down in here," Roland thundered. "What do you think we're looking for?"

Mark shrugged. "Not a clue, nor does Mrs. Davis. Though, she thinks it might be land developers looking for anything that would make the zoning or permitting illegal. Said that before the library was registered as a historical landmark, there'd been interest in demolishing it to make way for commercial property."

"Sounds about right," Anna cut in softly, her gold topaz eyes sparkling in the scattered light. "Most developers don't care about classic buildings like these, even though they try to imitate them. It's easier to knock them down and start from scratch, so they meet code."

Mark, Roland, and Townsend all turned to Anna at the same time, as if wondering where she'd come up with this information. The woman rarely spoke two words unless it involved actual *bag-worthy* evidence.

Anna shrugged. "My father owns a construction company. Although he loves old buildings and trees, he admits that more often than not it's easier to start from scratch. But I doubt seriously that even if developers found something that wasn't up to code, it would change the library's *historical landmark* status. After all, few old buildings are up to code. So as long as no remodeling is involved, that is hardly an issue."

Roland waved his hand around the room. "And yet, it's obvious, someone is looking for something. Kids have no reason to do this. And if I were a kid, why would I come back a second night? Why not trash other parts of the library? Why wouldn't they mess with something expensive like the computers up front if they really wanted to cause property damage?"

Mark nodded. "Good point, Roland," he offered, then glanced at Townsend. "Any thoughts?"

Townsend rubbed his thumb and index finger down both sides of his mustache, ending at the bottom of his mouth. "Maybe they left something in a reference book but can't remember which one it is."

So as not to appear condescending, Mark held his comment at bay and just nodded. Townsend didn't need to hear that was an excellent point; he'd been a damn good detective back in the day. He'd even been an invaluable training officer. Mark had learned a lot from him. He'd just been passed up for promotions because of his lackadaisical attitude and personal issues. "I think you're right, Townsend." Mark cocked his head to Roland. "Not sure what you're looking for, but bag anything you find. We'll take turns watching your back so you can work. This place is still large enough that someone could be hiding."

Roland walked off shaking his head, obviously overwhelmed at the task in front of him. He got paid whether he sat behind a desk or rummaged through dusty books, so Mark was certain he'd rather have his feet propped up while he tapped away on his smart phone.

Anna offered Mark a hint of a smile, then followed her superior to the first cleared shelves of books.

Mark really needed to clear the air with her, let her know he had no interest. At the same time, though, if she was just being nice, he'd feel like an idiot. The difference between men and women, it seemed. Women could flirt all they wanted and then claim innocence. But if a man flirted with a woman who wasn't interested, she could shoot him down whether it was innocent flirting or not and even claim workplace harassment if she wanted.

Anna's smiles were innocent enough. He just hated the smug look on Townsend's face that asked without words if he was going to follow through on Anna's flirtatious actions, knowing how Ashlyn would feel if it ever got back to her. Townsend's suggestion that

The Library

Mark take up with every pretty girl they came across was irritating. Surprisingly enough he hadn't made comments about Jay the librarian yet. Mark could only imagine what Townsend would say once he realized Mark had met her.

A rap at the front entrance interrupted whatever Townsend had planned to say, and Mark was grateful, but still confused, knowing it was Captain Davis. Mark opened the door, and Davis strolled in, heading directly to the reference area.

"Waters," Captain called over his shoulder, "you and Townsend start running down leads. I'll hang out with Roland and Anna and see what they come up with."

Mark stood at the entrance speechless. He certainly couldn't question a direct order, even though he wanted to. And yes, he'd be bored to tears sitting around all day as forensics bagged evidence. And sure, he could do a lot more good questioning potential witnesses. But since when did Davis start showing up at crime scenes and taking over his investigation?

CHAPTER 8

After a few hours of watching Roland and Anna bag everything from slips of paper to an unopened band-aid someone had used as a bookmark, Captain Andrew Davis headed to see the old man's body.

Andrew took his last deep breath before opening the door that led to the morgue. As usual, the room was cold and dreary. As many times as he'd been here over the years, it was amazing that he hadn't gotten used to it.

The M.E., Rick Cooper, glanced up when he tapped on the doorframe. "Captain, come on in. Still no ID, but I got your John Doe cleaned up, so at least we can get some images without the dirt-covered face and beard. Maybe a relative will step forward, since he has no teeth and no fingerprints."

Andrew glanced down at the lifeless body of the man the police had been hunting for twenty-eight years, the man he would recognize no matter how bedraggled and filthy he'd made himself.

Andrew had only been on the force a couple of years when he'd worked the double-homicide scene. He'd been the first officer on scene, since he'd been patrolling the neighborhood — Jessica's neighborhood.

He stepped away from the table, hoping to catch even the slightest amount of fresh air before speaking. "No need. Name's Wade Buchanan; his friends called him Buck." Andrew shook his head. Buchanan hadn't given Detective Wilson Waters a chance to clear him. Instead, he'd disappeared without a trace. There'd been talk back then that Buchanan had just settled a huge business deal and had skipped town with the money. Although that theory hadn't gone over well with Wilson Waters as motive for murdering his beautiful wife and daughter, it was the only conclusion the department and the general public were left with.

When Andrew was a teenager, he'd liked Buchanan. He'd even looked forward to the man becoming his father-in-law someday. Until his daughter had broken up with him because she was going away to college, that is. He had insisted that he'd wait for Jessica. But when she'd returned home for spring break the next year, she was on the arm of Gregory Burke. Andrew and Burke had gotten along okay in school, but Burke had turned into a pompous ass their senior year. The guy had even broken up with Laura Allan, the prettiest girl in school, even though the two of them had been dating for several years.

Andrew had never told Mark Waters that he'd had a crush on Ashlyn's mother in high school. All the guys had. After all, she'd been crowned Homecoming and Prom Queen. Not that he stood a chance of competing with Burke's wealth and stature. But then, Burke had broken it off with her, and Laura had turned into a real bitch. Then Burke comes back and moves in on his girl, Jessica, who actually looked a lot like Laura.

Jessica Buchanan had been working at the library the summer before she was going off for her graduate degree, and he had just been a lowly cop. He'd still been in love with her and would have taken her back in a heartbeat, but he'd caught wind that she was going to marry Gregory Burke.

The most ironic occurrence was that Andrew had

met his wife while working the case. For the life of him, he couldn't imagine why Margaret hadn't mentioned Buchanan's name the other day when she found him at the Library. No way hadn't she recognized Buchanan. And she'd known that he'd dated Buchanan's daughter and that the man had been wanted for murder for twenty-eight years. So why wouldn't she have said anything? Did she think he was still that upset with Buchanan, or had his wife had another reason for not admitting she'd recognized the man who tried to demolish her beloved library twenty-eight years ago?

CHAPTER 9

Ashlyn pushed the peas around her plate. She hated peas, especially faded and tasteless canned peas that looked more like round lima beans, which she also hated. She'd told her mother she wasn't hungry, but she'd forced the food on her anyway. If her mother cooked anything like her grandmother, she probably wouldn't have minded. Her mother hadn't inherited that gene or any of her grandmother's genetics as far as Ashlyn could tell. Nor her grandfather's for that matter.

Though Ashlyn was young when her grandfather had died, she remembered that he'd always been kind and sweet to her. And he always smelled like peppermint. A smile inched its way up her cheek at the memory. One of the few times he'd been well enough to play with her, he'd been chasing her around the house. But she'd stopped abruptly when she heard him wheeze, thinking he might have hurt his heart, as her grandmother had always reminded him not to do.

Ashlyn had never had a father figure, so she'd appreciated every minute she had with him and was just as happy curling up beside him as he worked crossword puzzles.

"What's funny, dear?" Her mother's voice snapped her from her happy memories of her grandparents.

Ashlyn shook her head, not wanting to explain that she was appreciating one of the few cheerful times of her childhood.

Her mother dropped her fork on her plate, the clink so loud that Ashlyn would be surprised not to find a chip in her grandmother's fine china. "Why must you shut me out of everything, Ashlyn?"

Ashlyn couldn't have suppressed a sigh if she tried, so she released it at the same time she rested her fork gently on her napkin, and then glared up at her mother. She released another breath that ended up coming out like a chuckle. Though clearly, there was no humor in her. "Me, shut you out?" She wiped her mouth and pushed her plate away. "That's rich, Mom, considering you shut me out of your emotions years ago."

Ashlyn scooted her chair across the hardwood floor, hoping she didn't leave a gouge, and used the table as support to push her body to a standing position. Getting vertical was a difficult task these days with her belly feeling as though she were carrying around a sack of potatoes.

Once standing, she leaned against the table and addressed her mother again, "When have you ever asked me how I felt?" Feeling a tear threaten to escape, she lifted her chin and sucked in a breath. "You know … every time I see pregnant women in pictures and movies, I always see their family around them, touching their belly, smiling, looking at silly ultrasound photos, even if they can't make out heads or tails of the black-and-white grainy photos. But you, nothing! You haven't even asked me if I found out if the baby is a boy or girl, or when my due date is. So don't try to say I shut you out."

Ashlyn barely felt finished, thinking she could go on for days, but knew it wasn't healthy for the baby, so she sucked in one final breath, determined to finish and go to bed. "You've never cared about me. I've been nothing but an inconvenience to you."

The Library

Her mother leapt to her feet. "That's not true!" Her mother had always been in tiptop shape. At fifty-one, she could easily still pass for her forties. "Do you know how hard it was being a single mother?"

Ashlyn couldn't resist rolling her eyes. "No, Mom. Funny, I don't think you've ever told me how hard it was to be a single mother. You mean the fact that you lost an acting job, or that you drove your husband to the grave, or the million-dollar insurance policy you got, or the daughter who allowed you to drag her around from one beauty pageant to another for years, or the time your daughter was ungrateful and asked that you stop." Ashlyn crossed her arms and glowered at her. "Oh, I know, it was the slew of men you had to entertain overnight for years. Some of which made passes at me when I was only thirteen, the reason I no longer wanted to be your dress-up doll. So, which one of those was hardest on you, Mom?"

Her mother let out a long sigh and sat back down, shaking her head. "You have no idea, Ashlyn."

"No. I guess I don't." Ashlyn turned to leave, deciding she'd pack up and go home first thing in the morning. Yes, she loved the house and the memory of her grandparents. But as long as her mother was here, it wasn't a good environment for her.

"Wait."

Ashlyn stopped, even though she didn't want to. She was still her mother, as her aunt always reminded her, and she was to treat her mother respectfully. No, she didn't have to take her verbal attacks, but she had no right to attack back. *It takes two*, her aunt had always lovingly reminded her.

"I'm sorry, honey. I know I haven't been open with you, but that's because I've been hurt too. I just didn't want to tell you, but maybe I should have."

"Now?" Ashlyn groaned. She should have known that she couldn't have said anything without her mother trying to one-up her. Far as she knew, no one had ever attacked her mother and left her for dead. What could be worse than that? She was sure her mother would come up with some outlandish story if she let her. "I'm too tired, Mom."

Her mother shook her head, a small smile cracking her perfectly made-up face. "I remember those days. I felt like a hippo when I was pregnant with you. I'd been so careful not to gain weight, but it didn't matter; I just kept growing and growing."

Ashlyn stepped back a few steps and lowered herself onto the Waverly-fabric covered sofa, letting her mother know without speaking that she welcomed this conversation. Not once in Ashlyn's twenty-three years had her mother ever mentioned anything loving or funny about her pregnancy. Just that she'd lost a great movie role.

Her mother sat in the chair across from her. "When you were born, I was surprised that you were so small. How could you be so tiny when I gained almost forty pounds?"

Ashlyn smiled. "I wasn't that little. I was seven pounds and seven ounces if I remember correctly?"

"Yep. My mother said you were lucky. That you had God's number on you."

"That sounds like something Mémé would say."

Her mother nodded. "My mother was a good woman. I'm sorry that I haven't been more like her."

"Mom ..." Ashlyn whined. Just when she thought they might have been able to have an adult conversation, her mother had to ruin it. "I've told you this before. I don't want to rehash the past, but you forced me by making that ridiculous comment. I've told you, if you want to start fresh, we can try, but I'll be damned if I'll allow you to blame me for your lack of stardom or whatever it is you wanted. I've made mistakes. Look at me! I'm eight months pregnant, the father's dead, I haven't told his parents, and I keep pushing away the greatest man I've ever known so I can work out all my problems on my own — and don't you dare say a word about Mark," she added when she heard her mother take a breath. "I swear to you if you utter one negative word about him, I'll walk out of this house right now. He's the best thing that's ever happened to me."

"I wasn't going to say anything about Mark, honey. I can see he's a great man, and that's some engagement ring."

Ashlyn looked down at the ring that her mother hadn't uttered a word about until now. "It is. I don't know what he was thinking ... buying me something this extravagant."

"He loves you. I think that's obvious. How many men would be willing to marry a woman carrying another man's —" She stopped when Ashlyn glared at her. "Sorry, but it's true."

"I know," Ashlyn conceded. "He asked if I wanted to break up. I don't want to break up; I just want to clear my head. I'm afraid, Mom. I'm afraid they'll try to take my baby."

Her mother released a long sigh. "I wish you had told me you were dating Devin Burke. I would have warned you away from him."

The Library

Ashlyn narrowed her eyes in confusion. "What do you mean?"

"I dated his father, Gregory Burke, all through high school."

"Excuse me? You did what?" Ashlyn shrilled, struggling to push herself off the deep indent of the old sofa. "You dated Devin Burke's father? The grandfather of my baby?"

Her mother's head dropped to her chest. "Yes. All through high school."

Ashlyn dropped her head too and shook it back and forth. "No wonder you want me to tell them. And I thought — no, no ... I always knew you had ulterior motives for pushing me. But revenge, Mom? That's even beneath you."

"It's not like that, Ashlyn." Her mother stood up and took her hand, effectively keeping Ashlyn from storming to her room. "Well, maybe a little like it, I guess. But mostly ... I just want Gregory to own up to what that beast tried to do to you. And he owes you support. And your baby is the only heir to their fortune now that Devin is dead."

Ashlyn dropped her head in her hands. "Oh, my God, Mother. This is all such a mess, and now my baby's grandparents have another reason to hate me and fight me for custody." She looked up at her mother. "What happened? How did you break up? Was it a bad break?"

For the first time Ashlyn could ever remember, Laura Allan had real tears in her eyes. She couldn't ever remember seeing her cry. Even at Mémé's death, her mother had cried crocodile tears.

"I don't know." Her mother leaned against the arm of the sofa and pulled a pillow onto her lap. "We'd dated all through high school. We had a few spats here and there, mostly because he never introduced me to his parents. But I understood. He said they'd just make trouble for us. They already had a wealthy girl they wanted him to date, but she was younger. He'd promised that we'd elope right after high school, and then it'd be too late for them to stop us. But right after prom, he drove me home." She released a deep breath and wiped away a tear. "I thought that we'd continue the evening." Her mother peeked up. "You know ... I thought he would have rented us a hotel room. I'd already told him my mother thought I was staying at a friend's house. But he parked in front of my house, didn't even bother pulling into the driveway, and asked for his school ring back, insisting we were over."

"Wow ..." Ashlyn finally interrupted. "This is

sounding a lot like what happened between Devin and me. Only Devin didn't want a ring, he wanted me to abort my baby."

"That's what I mean, Ashlyn. I really loved Gregory, and I'm sure he loved me. And then when you told me what happened, and that Devin was the baby's father, well, I guess it just seemed odd."

Ashlyn ran her hand through her hair, twisting it and then draping it over her shoulder, holding it as if it were her lifeline. Now she wasn't sure what she should do. "I need to go back home, I guess. Talk to Mark."

Her mother nodded.

"I'm not sure what I'm going to do. I certainly don't care about their money, but I feel as though I'm not being fair to my son. If he has grandparents, he should be able to meet them." She looked back at her mother. "Is Gregory Burke a good man?"

Her mother took in a deep breath and then let it whoosh out in one long exhale. "He was, honey. But something changed. After he broke up with me, he started dating the woman his parents wanted for him. She was a year younger than we were. But then her father murdered her, and Gregory was never the same." Ashlyn gasped, and her mother just nodded. "It was horrible. I tried to talk to Gregory when I found out, but he refused to see me. After that, he turned into a ruthless businessman, just like his father and grandfather, even though he'd never wanted to be like them, swore that he had no desire for their life. Now he owns just about every piece of commercial property in Edenbury."

CHAPTER 10

Mark followed Jay down the long row of books, watching as she pulled individual titles out and then deftly placed them back in their niche. As hard as he focused, he couldn't make out the different names of the novels, though.

Her hair wasn't up anymore; instead, it flowed around her shoulders and halfway down her back in a fiery blaze of curls. Her long skirt billowed behind her as she flitted along the aisles, holding up book after book as though she were appraising each one.

Why had she brought him here? And more importantly, why was he here? He didn't want to be here, but he couldn't help but follow her through the darkness, hoping she'd reveal something that would contribute to his case.

He inhaled deeply, relishing the earthy scent of the library as well as the ever-present fragrance of jasmine. The glabrous green-leafed vines with clusters of white flowers had worked their way through the stone and beveled glass on the second floor of the ancient structure, slipping through the cracks and finding a home among the old books that lined the shelves.

An opaque mist rose from the wood floor and circled his legs, slowly crawling up the lower half of his body. The dense vapor worked its way up his chest, separating into strips of smoke. The snowy-white tendrils of the fog stretched into fingers, then entwined in his hair, surrounding his neck and slowly pulling him toward Jay.

"Mark ..." Jay whispered in his ear. Her cool breath caressed his neck, sending shivers down his spine.

"No!" Mark shouted, bolting upright in bed. "Oh, God!" He expelled a long breath, his heart pounding as if he'd had a nightmare. He fell back onto the bed, punching the pillow beneath his head and jerking the blanket up to his chin.

It was no use. He wouldn't be able to fall back asleep. Why in the world would he be fantasizing

The Library

about Jay? Well, he wasn't really fantasizing. He hadn't thought of anything sexual — yet. He'd just been following her down the aisle of books. For some reason, his subconscious thought that maybe she could help him find what he was looking for, it seemed.

Still, he didn't like other women entering his dreams, even platonically. He wanted Ashlyn in his life and his dreams. He sat upright again and scooped his phone off the nightstand, glancing at the time. Four a.m.

"Great," he grumbled. He'd be exhausted by the end of the day.

He needed to question Jay. He'd given her enough time; it was time for answers. She had shut down on him almost immediately the other day, but it was clear she knew something. Even if she didn't know what secrets she possessed, she'd spent time with the old man, so he may have mentioned someone. Captain had called him with the ID, which matched what Jay had said. Buck, short for Buchanan.

The man had an outstanding warrant for arrest for the murders of his wife and daughter twenty-eight years ago. Had Jay known that about him? Mark understood that she would be polite to the homeless community, since they were in the library often. But why would a twenty-something-year-old college girl socialize to the point of playing board games? Yes, he definitely needed to have a conversation with Jay.

Decision made, Mark jumped out of bed and made a beeline for the shower. A cold shower would do his mind — he glanced down — and his body good.

Wide-eyed and anxious after his cold shower, he decided to text Ashlyn and let her know he was thinking about her — because he was. No matter what his mind was attempting to do in his dream, Ashlyn fulfilled his every fantasy. He simply didn't want anyone else — ever.

They had a lot to discuss, but he also had a murder to solve, so maybe it was better she was away. Mark hoped he wouldn't wake her, but once he got rolling, his mind would be occupied. He grabbed his phone and tapped out a few words: *Wanted you to know I'm thinking about you. Love you! C U Soon!* <3

"That should do it," he said to his calico as she curled around his legs. "Nothing too mushy, just the facts." She let out a long meow in response, which he accepted as agreement, even though she probably just wanted fed.

After feeding kitty — he'd never bothered to name

the cute rescue cat — he shoved his Glock into his specially made harness.

Since he dressed in plain clothes, he didn't want civilians questioning why he had a gun when he entered public buildings. The slim in-waist holster did a great job of hiding his weapon. Of course, anyone who gave him more than a cursory glance would finger him as a cop. Yeah, he was a detective, but he could never work UC. Captain had almost laughed when he'd requested working undercover on a few stings.

Though, when he was younger, Captain had allowed him to pick up a few streetwalkers when the taxpayers complained that the city needed to clean up the streets.

Most of the women had pinned him for a cop immediately. Only the more desperate hookers bought his story that he was just a lonely college kid looking for a good time with no strings attached. He assumed the captain — who'd been a lieutenant at the time — had been testing him.

Nothing he did would change it; he looked like a cop.

Mark grabbed his keys, wallet, radio, and cuffs off the kitchen counter, where he tossed them the moment he came home, and was heading out the door when his phone buzzed.

Hey, Babe! You're up early. I've been up all night talking with Mom. We made a major breakthrough in our relationship. Though, I don't know how long that'll last. I'm crashing now. Have a great day. I can't wait to see you. I love you! <3 <3 <3

Mark laughed. Ashlyn would never use abbreviations, even in a text. And, wow! Three hearts. It must have been a great breakthrough. He quickly responded: *Wonderful news! Get some sleep and call me later. Heading out.*

She responded with a smiley and a heart, which meant that she'd received the message, and the conversation was over. They'd both admitted how they hated it when the texts went back and forth because no one knew how to end the conversation, and agreed a smiley works wonders.

Mark decided his first stop would be the library. If there had been another break-in, Mark wanted to find the culprit first. He'd taken it upon himself to install new locks on all the doors yesterday and had kept a set of keys to do some additional investigating.

Changing locks wasn't in his job description, but

The Library

it hadn't been the first time he'd done it for a citizen. When he was on patrol, he'd worked the scene of a car theft. The woman was in her seventies and had been distressed. Not because of monetary loss, rather because she'd left her keys under the seat while she was inside the mall, since she had a keypad on the door. The thief not only had her car, he had her home address and keys to her house.

Understanding that she lived alone, Mark had driven her to Home Depot and then to her house and had changed all the locks. The city had given him a certificate of commendation, but he'd only seen it as his duty: to protect and serve.

It wasn't five yet, so the Pennsylvania sky was unlit, with barely even the light of the moon penetrating the dense cloud cover. As soon as he rounded the last corner near the library, Mark extinguished all the lights on his cruiser, shifted the vehicle into neutral, turned off the ignition, and coasted within a hundred feet of the building. He smoothly parked his unmarked car along the curb and got out of the vehicle, barely touching the door to the jamb.

Instead of walking up the sidewalk, Mark crossed the narrow concrete and turned onto a side street that ran beside the old structure. Eyeing the back alley, his gaze darted back and forth as he crept toward the old building.

The library wasn't the only historic construction on the street. One building after another, all in the same medina stone, lined the entire block. Even an old church with an ancient clock tower that no longer chimed and a remodeled fire station resembled the outside walls of the library.

It wasn't the greatest area of town, but Mark had always enjoyed driving through it, appreciating the nostalgic feel of the mammoth creations, all with intricate carved patterns and elaborate windows and moldings. Modern-day configurations just didn't offer the same appeal.

He wasn't, however, in the habit of searching a building without backup. He hoped the fact that the sun was almost up at least meant that most of the drunks — who were the worst criminals to deal with — would have already passed out. When he was a uniformed officer, he'd learned that he could reason with just about anyone but a plastered fool.

Mark easily hopped the three-foot-high black-iron gate, which kept wanderers from trouncing across the green lawn, and padded his way up the grassy knoll toward the rear of the edifice. If he were a bad guy planning to break in, he'd go to the rear doors. He'd recognized years ago that in order to be a good cop, he had to think like a criminal.

A long screech, then inaudible whispers had Mark drawing his Glock. He inched his way along the outside wall just as a man was closing and locking the gate that surrounded the patio. He saw several people disappear around the hedge behind the library, but didn't dare shout out and alert the man in front of him.

With one bound from behind the green shrub, Mark shoved the man against the gate, immediately wrenching one of his arms behind his back, then the other. "Police! You're under arrest for trespassing."

The man didn't resist, so Mark unsnapped the leather clip on his belt and retrieved his cuffs. He snapped the metal over each wrist, then turned the man toward him. "Who're your friends?"

"No one."

"Of course." Mark looked down at the man's soiled hands, still holding a key. "Where d'ya get that key?"

"Friend."

"You got any weapons or drugs on ya? Needles?"

"Nuh-uh. Don't do drugs."

Mark carefully patted the man down, careful not to stick himself in the event the man had lied, which was a pretty safe bet, since most of the people he arrested lied. He took the key and unlocked the gate, still holding onto the man's arm. "What were ya doin' on private property?"

"Nothin'. Just hangin' out with friends."

Glancing around, Mark couldn't see any signs of a break-in, but he walked to the rear door, dragging the man along, and checked, rattling both doors. Solid. "You been inside?"

"Not ter'nite."

"Last night?"

"No, sir. Only in da day."

Mark nodded, his gaze raking across the area. "So, what were you doing here?"

"Told ya. Just hangin' out."

"Did you know Buck?"

The man responded only with a nod.

"Let's go." Mark maneuvered the man around and pushed him forward. Dammit! He didn't think to get a key to the surrounding gate, and there was no way the man would be able to hop the gate while handcuffed. He reached in his pocket for the key he'd taken from the man. Maybe. He slipped the key into the gate and sure enough, it unlatched easily.

"Where d'ya get this key, mister?" Mark asked again.

"Told ya. A friend."

Mark pushed the man through the opening, keeping a continual watch of his surroundings, wondering where the man's *friends* went. "Looks like your *friends* dumped you. Some friends."

The man harrumphed in response, but offered nothing else, so Mark led him down the street to his patrol car.

Before opening the door, he did a more thorough pat down, since he didn't have a cage in his vehicle. "Got ID?" Mark asked when he didn't find a wallet.

"No, sir. Don't need one."

"Gotta name?"

"Bill."

Of course, Mark thought.

Tired of the one and two-word answers, Mark placed his hand on the man's head and directed him into the car. He pressed a hard forearm against the man's head, pinning him to the seat while he strapped him in. Safer than him coming across the seat if he decided to go psycho inside the car once they started moving.

"Don't let me hear the click of the seatbelt

unsnapping," Mark warned. "You're a big guy, so I'd have to defend myself. I don't like to use deadly force, but I will if I have to. Understand?"

Bill nodded that he understood.

Mark had learned a long time ago to speak their language and let them know he meant business. He never used unnecessary force, but made sure offenders knew he would. Amazing how quickly just the threat of force terminated most situations.

Before driving to the station, Mark weaved his way up and down several side streets to see where the man's friends had gone. Like most vagrants, they'd scurried away and hidden in the shadows, out of his sight.

More than likely, the man didn't know anything, but he was still trespassing, even if he had a key.

Mark pulled into the station and led the man straight to an interview room without booking him. He'd hold the charge of trespassing as a wild card. Mark went for coffee while leaving Bill to wait. Not that he thought that would gain him an edge — obviously this wasn't the homeless man's first arrest — but because Mark needed coffee. He wished it wasn't the crappy stuff he'd been drinking for the last few days; but caffeine was still caffeine, and he needed it.

He really needed to start brewing his coffee at home, since he never seemed to have time to pick some up once he left his apartment.

Mark made a quick stop at his office, hoping Townsend had arrived. The man was behind his desk all right, but his head was on the blotter. Drool had already caused a few marked entries on the pad to bleed across the paper. Mark shook his head. Yeah, he'd been sleeping here.

"Townsend," Mark said at the same time he rapped on the older detective's cubicle entrance.

Townsend jumped in response. "What the —" He wiped his eyes, which were swollen and red.

Sad. If he'd stop being such a horndog, maybe his wife would keep him. She'd sure taken him back enough times.

Mark leaned against the cubicle wall, waiting as Townsend got his bearings. "I need you to track down some of the homeless community today. Find out if anyone saw anything."

Townsend wiped at his eyes some more as he stretched, but nodded. "Yup. Got anything I can start with?"

"Mention a guy named Bill, tall gangly fella. I have

him in custody for trespassing. Several of his friends saw me arrest him, so let them assume he's talking."

"Got it." Townsend blinked his eyes, as if he were trying to wake up, and then motioned his head to the styrofoam cups Mark held. "You drinking both of those?"

"One's for Bill."

His partner grunted.

When Mark returned to his detainee, he handed Bill the cup of coffee, read him his rights, offered if he wanted an attorney — which he declined — and then peppered him with the same questions he'd asked the man earlier.

The only thing that changed from outside the library was that he got his full name William "Wild Bill" James.

"So, Bill …" Mark smiled, attempting to get the man to let down his guard. "Why d'your friends call you Wild Bill?"

Bill shrugged and flashed a nicotine-stained grin. Surprisingly, his teeth weren't rotting away as he'd seen with most of the homeless community. "No reason other than my name is Bill. Like the Old West, Wild Bill Hickok. Some folks say I look like him."

Mark tilted his head, taking in the long dark hair,

which hung in greasy and stringy strands with a bit of a wave. Bill had thin brows above wide-set narrow eyes and a long thin nose. "Hmm ... you kinda do."

"And the fact that I was a cop back in the day."

"Really? What day was that?" Mark asked.

"Long before you, kid." The man's street lingo had almost completely disappeared.

Mark dropped his head and stared at the man, realizing he'd seen him before. He wagged his finger as it occurred to him. "I saw you the other day. You were talking with Jay on the second floor of the library."

Bill shook his head. "Don't know no Jay."

"Yeah, you do. I saw you. The young librarian," Mark clarified. "The redhead."

The man nodded in acknowledgment, but then shook his head. "She may have been talking to me, but I wasn't talking to her. I don't talk to her."

CHAPTER 11

Andrew Davis squinted against the first rays of sunlight, watching as his wife of almost twenty-five years tiptoed to their bedroom door.

"Where ya going, Margaret?" Andrew asked. She'd been gone a lot lately, and it made him wonder what she'd been doing, since he'd instructed her not to open the library until he concluded his investigation.

They'd been happy for the most part. Their lives had just gravitated together after Jessica's death, but he'd always tried to be a good husband. Margaret knew she wasn't his first choice for a wife, but she also didn't try to compete with a dead woman, the only woman he'd ever truly loved. They'd had their issues over the

The Library

years, but had worked out most of them and had fallen into a comfortable pattern.

Although he'd never love her as much as Jessica, he did love and care for her. He'd also learned to read her well in the last two and a half decades, and it was clear; his wife was keeping something from him.

She jumped at the sound of his voice, obviously surprised that he was up so early, but then again, so was she — again.

"Oh!" she gasped. "You startled me."

He wiggled his eyebrows at her, wondering if she'd be up for a quickie. "Save the librarian charm for the groupies. I know you're a tiger."

She smiled, a hint of pink highlighting her pale cheeks, but she didn't make her way back to the bed, so she really was in a hurry to get somewhere. "I want to get to the library early in case there was another break-in."

He shook his head. "I told you yesterday, the library is now a crime scene. When the scene was outside, I gave in. You opened when I said you shouldn't and look what happened. What if the intruder had still been there when you arrived?"

"But," she huffed, planting her hands on her hips,

"we need to open. We have enough issues. We don't need citizens complaining to the city council."

"At five a.m.?" He scooted up in the bed and propped his chin on his fist, narrowing his eyes. "By the way, why did I have to find out for myself that Wade Buchanan was hanging out at the library, Margaret?" he asked her point-blank, wondering what she knew about the man showing up after twenty-eight years of being in hiding.

It made no sense that she wouldn't confide in him that a man wanted for two murders was stalking the library. At minimum, unless she had a good reason for keeping quiet, she would have told Buchanan to leave the premises.

She released a deep breath and leaned against the doorframe. Still in the room, but as far from him as she could get. "You know I hated Wade Buchanan, but I never believed he murdered his wife and daughter."

"I know you never liked him. He was hell-bent on bulldozing the library. But how can you be so sure he didn't kill his family?"

She shrugged. "I just know."

"Were you worried I'd turn him in or try to hurt him if I discovered he was hanging around the library?"

The Library

His wife licked her lips before answering, which meant she was either dehydrated from sleep or preparing to lie. "Both," she croaked out.

Hmm, he mused silently. Her one-word answer didn't sound like a lie. Unless she was holding something back. Whether people realized it or not, their bodies gave away an omission of the truth just as much as if they'd actually lied.

He didn't want to badger his wife, but he did want to know how much she knew about the Buchanan murders. It had been a long twenty-eight years since Buchanan had disappeared. Of course, no one in the police department had been looking closely for him.

After Wilson Waters died, most of his investigations got swept to the side. It was amazing, though, that Buchanan had managed to hide in this small town for so long. Someone had to have helped him.

Why would Margaret have wanted to keep a possible murderer out of jail? Unless she had proof that he was innocent.

His wife knew one truth; he hated Wade Buchanan too, and he always would. Jessica would still be alive if she'd stayed with him.

CHAPTER 12

After interviewing Wild Bill for three hours, Mark finally let him go with a stiff warning not to return to the library after hours and to stay in town in the event he had further questions.

Not that Mark thought Bill had the means of skipping town quickly, but even a slow pace could have him in the next county before nightfall. Or hitchhiking — the preferred method among most vagrants — would have him in another state in a few hours.

Fortunately, even without family, the homeless community still fell into comfortable patterns and preferred not to relocate. They knew where to find food, shelter, and which areas to avoid. A new city

The Library

meant more work just to be safe. Wild Bill didn't look as though he'd been on the streets long, though, so more than likely, he'd stick around.

The library was still closed, per Captain Davis' orders, so Mark headed back there, hoping to do some investigating on his own. Roland and Anna had finished their search yesterday evening and hadn't found anything interesting.

Plenty of scribbled notes in margins and sticky notes pasted to pages, but nothing that screamed "secret information," Roland had told him over the phone when the team left at nine p.m. Regardless, they'd bagged everything they found for Mark to sift through when he was ready.

"Tomorrow," Roland had grudgingly told him during their phone call, "I'll scan the microfilm per your request. Thanks for that, Waters. I owe you one," he'd complained.

"Anytime, man," Mark had responded. "Think of it this way, maybe you'll solve a twenty-eight-year-old murder and a current murder case simultaneously, earning you the coveted position of city employee of the month. I think you even get a fifty-dollar gift card to a steakhouse with your plaque."

"Hah! I'll leave the solving murders to you guys;

I just provide the information. All I see in my near future is a cold beer and a night spent laughing at the wannabe cops on TV, and in the not-so-distant future, retirement."

Roland had hung up after that with the assurance that he'd be veggin' on the sofa for the rest of the evening. The older gentleman was the type of man you couldn't help but like. He looked nothing like a scientist. He was tall and burly; a man you'd expect was a lumberjack at one time in his life, not a forensic scientist.

Now that the sun was long up, and Mark doubted anyone would be desperate enough to break in during the day, he parked near the main gate in front of the library.

The woman held his gaze from the moment he shifted the vehicle into park until he stood in front of her.

"You ready to talk, Jay ..." He let her first name fade off his tongue, again hoping she'd fill in the blank.

She didn't. Instead, she stood up and walked around the bench, making her way toward the front door. "You have a key, I hope."

Mark nodded. "I do. Are you ready to talk to me?"

"Let's go inside."

The Library

For whatever reason, Mark felt uncomfortable, as if this twenty-something, barely a hundred-ten-pound girl could be a threat. But, he had a Glock strapped to his side, and he doubted she had a thigh holster stuffed with a 9mm beneath the skirt she wore.

With hesitation, he followed her as she walked toward the stairs, but stopped at the landing. He'd been a cop long enough that he didn't trust anyone involved with a murder case, beautiful or not.

"Where're you going?" he asked as she sashayed up the stairs, passing a rectangular table next to the reference room, which still had Roland's yellow tape pasted across the doorway. The table would have served perfectly as an interview station. Long enough that she would be out of his reach, which would enable her to let down her guard.

She glanced over her shoulder but continued ascending the steps. "Upstairs. I told you I work in fiction."

Mark crossed his arms over his chest, refusing to follow. This was too similar to his dream for comfort. "I'd rather we talk right here," he called, watching as she glided onto the second-floor landing with the gracefulness of a ballerina.

She leaned over the railing and grinned. "Are you afraid the ghost might get you?"

He frowned. One, he wasn't afraid of anything, least of all a ghost, well, maybe slightly. Ghostly beings — whatever they were — had been known to entice people to do stupid things. And two, if someone else had known about a presence in the library, why wouldn't he have heard rumors about it all the years he'd been coming here?

He'd insinuated to Ashlyn that he hadn't heard details about the ghost that haunted The Depot. When, in fact, he'd heard of disturbances for years from the police officers who'd had to go to calls at three a.m. Townsend was the worst; he hardly even wanted to eat lunch there anymore.

"What ghost?" he ventured, taking one tentative step at a time toward the young woman.

"I saw your expression the other day. Something happened, didn't it?"

"I don't believe in ghosts," he grumbled, still slogging up the stairs like a child heading toward a punishment.

Jay giggled. "Just because you don't believe in ghosts doesn't mean they don't exist."

Mark stepped off the last step onto the smooth

wood floors and leaned against the banister. "First question, Jay. Why are you here?"

"I volunteer here, remember?" She turned and strolled toward the rows of books, trailing her hand along the spines. She flitted from one shelf to the next as if she were admiring each individual book. As tiny as she was, he couldn't imagine that even with the ladders she could reach the books on the top shelves. Each shelf touched the twelve-foot-high ceiling.

No wonder they needed someone to work in the different sections. He couldn't imagine that they allowed patrons to climb the ladders to reach books on the top shelves. If a person fell from that distance, it was doubtful they'd walk away uninjured. More than likely, they'd die of head trauma.

Mark glanced toward the stained-glass windows, confirming that the vines from the patio hadn't worked their way through the cracks as they'd done in his dream. He let out a breath of relief when the window frames appeared solid.

Jay finally stopped prancing around and sat in a chair at the end of the aisle, leaving him to stand. "This is my favorite place in the library."

Mark glanced around, noticing she was sandwiched between stacks of books, a wall behind her with no place to go, and that the only exit would be to come through him. He wouldn't feel comfortable without a means of escape, but maybe she felt safe within her cocoon of books.

"How did you know I'd be here?" he continued his questioning.

She pulled her legs closer, as though attempting to hide them beneath the chair. "I didn't, but I'd hoped."

"Mrs. Davis said she would call all the employees and instruct them not to come in."

"I'm not an employee; I'm a volunteer. And I don't have a phone, remember?"

He nodded. "Do you know William James, goes by Wild Bill?"

"Not personally. He started hanging out with Buck a few months ago. They seemed to have gotten awfully friendly, though."

"I saw you speaking to Bill the other day. What did you discuss?"

"I asked him if he knew who killed Buck."

Mark leaned against the shelves, hoping they were sturdy enough to hold his weight. "Did he?"

"He wouldn't talk to me."

"Why not? Didn't he know you and Buck were friends?"

The Library

Jay shrugged. "I think so, but some homeless people don't like to talk."

Mark nodded. He did know that. But though Bill had fed him a ton of one-word answers, when they were just shooting the breeze, he'd actually opened up. Maybe he was just concerned that someone might get the wrong idea witnessing a homeless man chatting with a beautiful young college volunteer.

Mark could understand that. Right now, he wasn't too comfortable with the current situation. Jay could turn around and accuse him of any type of misconduct, and whom would people believe? The captain's first question would be: why hadn't he brought her down to the station, knowing that he couldn't force anyone to go to the station or talk for that matter. If a witness was willing to talk, he listened, wherever it was.

"You know ... Buck didn't murder his family," Jay spouted off out of nowhere.

Mark huffed out a breath, not understanding why this young woman would have felt comfortable socializing with a man wanted for homicide. "And how exactly could you have been sure enough of that not to turn him in if you knew he was wanted for murder, Jay?"

"He told me," she answered simply.

The innocence in her voice made him want to believe as well, but he was far too cynical to trust a wanted criminal's pleas of innocence without proof. All criminals claimed they were innocent.

He scratched the scruff on his face that was beginning to itch from not shaving. "Oh ... well, that makes perfectly good sense then."

"If you'd heard him talk about his wife and daughter, you'd know he never could have hurt them."

Mark resisted rolling his eyes at her naïveté. Many people loved their family and still killed them. That's why those types of murders were referred to as crimes of passion, but he didn't bother stating the obvious. Instead, he asked, "Did he happen to mention who killed them, then?"

"He said it was one of four people, but he was never sure. When he came home the night of his family's murder, someone knocked him out. When he woke up and found the bodies, he realized immediately that he'd be the prime suspect. So instead of running to the police, he grabbed his daughter's key to the library, knowing he could hide within the walls until he figured out who did it —" She stopped abruptly, glancing around at her shelter of books, as if wondering if she'd said too much.

At least Mark now knew how Buck had been able to get into the patio area of the library after hours. But how had Bill gotten the key? Had he taken it from Buck after he murdered him? If so, why would Bill have come back to the scene of the crime? Unless he was the one who'd been trashing the library. But for what? What could a homeless man be looking for in the reference section? And what information could get Buck killed twenty-eight years after his family had been murdered?

Needing more info, Mark pressed Jay for the people Buck had supposedly mentioned. "Did he tell you who the four people were?"

Jay glanced up at him, her honey-colored eyes seeming to shelter a secret she didn't want to release. "You'll never believe me if I tell you, Mark."

Mark tilted his head in confusion. The familiar way she referred to him was unnerving. And why wouldn't he believe her? "Try me."

Jay ran her fingers over the spine of a book next to her, caressing it with a gentle touch, as if she could draw strength with just a stroke of her fingertips. "If I tell you, you have to promise that you'll never mention my name."

"I'll need you to testify if I make an arrest."

"We'll cross that bridge when we get there, but you have to swear you won't mention my name to anyone, especially those involved, and you can't write my name in any reports while you investigate the case. And whatever you do, don't mention to Mrs. Davis that I spoke to you."

Mark narrowed his eyes, but nodded. He'd dealt with plenty of CIs over the years. "Okay. But I can't stop the courts from issuing a court order for you to testify."

"Just don't write my name on any paperwork until you make an arrest."

"Okay," he acquiesced, knowing he didn't have a choice if he wanted her to talk to him. She was obviously scared for some reason.

Jay clasped her hands and rested them in her lap. "First of all, did Andrew Davis tell you he dated Buck's daughter all through high school?"

Knowing it was never smart to interrupt a witness, Mark shook his head and attempted to keep the shock off his face. No. Captain Davis had failed to mention that tidbit of information over the phone last night.

The Library

The moment he'd been made aware of the victim's ID, he should have offered that information. Mark held his gaze steady while he waited for Jay to continue.

"Buck was in a lucrative business deal with Gregory Burke, who had just taken over his father's business. His family was one of the wealthiest landowners in town, and he just so happened to start dating Buck's daughter after she'd broken up with Andrew."

"Wait," Mark interrupted. "Gregory Burke of *the* Burkes?"

"Yes. Gregory had dated Laura Allan all through high school but broke up with her his senior year and pursued Jessica, Buck's daughter, per his family's insistence."

"That's enough!" Mark shouted. "Who put you up to this?"

Jay tilted her head as though confused. "Excuse me?"

"Laura Allan is my mother-in-law to be, Andrew Davis is my boss, and I just worked the death of Gregory Burke's son six months ago, and you're trying to tell me you just came up with all of those names off the top of your head, and they all have connections with a murder twenty-eight years ago?" He slammed his hand against the stack of books, feeling the sting, but not caring. "Next thing you'll tell me is that Mrs. Davis knows about all this."

Jay nodded. "Mrs. Davis would do anything to save her precious library, Mark."

CHAPTER 13

Mark slammed through Captain Davis' door, not concerned if anyone was on the other side. "What the fu —" He bit his tongue. Not needing to find himself suspended for insubordination, he continued but was still indignant. "What the hell is going on, Cap'n?"

Captain Davis calmly rose from his chair and walked around the desk without a word. He passed where Mark stood rooted in front of his desk and closed the door. He walked past Mark again and took his seat in his chair, narrowing his eyes. "Sit down, Waters," he bit out.

Mark didn't want to sit, but he did as ordered. Though he didn't sit respectfully. Instead, he plopped down onto the soft leather and crossed his arms in defiance. He couldn't wait to hear Davis' explanation.

Davis steepled his fingers, resting his elbows on the desk. "What exactly is it that you think you know, Waters?"

Mark chewed on the inside of his lip, a smile threatening, as he watched the captain attempt to belittle him with his body language. Mark uncrossed his arms and leaned back in the chair, watching as his superior mirrored his actions. "Why don't you just start at the beginning, Cap'n?"

Davis let out a chuckle in response.

Tit for tat. *This wasn't going to go well*, Mark realized. How would he interview the man who had taught him how to interview a suspect? His best bet was to keep quiet, he decided. Hope that Davis would want to clear his name of whatever he thought Mark had on him.

"I see you detained a suspect this morning," Captain said. "Didn't have enough to arrest him, though?"

"He wasn't a suspect. Just a vagrant I found wandering around the library. Nevertheless, we had an interesting conversation," Mark said, allowing Davis to assume what he wanted out of that scrap of information. Maybe he'd think Wild Bill had told him about Davis' connection to the case.

"Yeah. About what?"

Mark leaned forward. "You know, Cap'n, you slipped up the first morning at the library."

Davis leaned forward a fraction in response, but catching his automatic reaction, he busied himself with shuffling papers on his blotter. "I'm not hiding anything, Waters. Yeah, I knew Wade Buchanan, but I didn't want to identify him without being certain."

"Uh-uh, Cap'n. You knew it was Wade Buchanan before we even saw him. When I asked you if I could take Ashlyn's phone call, you said 'the old man,' as if you'd known him personally. As though you dated his daughter at one time." Mark inched forward another inch. "Now, do you want to talk to me, Cap'n, or do I need to start asking around?"

Captain Davis scratched his nose for a brief second then spit out, "Margaret told me it was an old man. I didn't kill Wade Buchanan, Mark. And until you have your facts clear, I suggest you be careful where you tread, Detective."

Mark released a long breath and nodded. "I'm not suggesting you killed anyone, Cap'n. But all of a sudden there are a lot of connections to you and your wife."

"Wild Bill tell you that? Strange that he's been gone for years, and all of a sudden just shows up in the last six months. Hanging around my wife's workplace." Davis nodded as if he were thinking about the situation, wondering how much to tell. "Yeah, I've been keeping my eye on him. Never trusted him. Wild Bill used to be a cop, but got canned for being on the take. Gambling problem. Owed a lot of debts. He was in good with the chief at the time, though. So his infractions had been overlooked a few times."

Mark nodded. There were always two sides to every story: the truth, and the way everyone else remembered the truth. Unfortunately, most people were revisionists. No one ever remembered all the facts of a story, only what best suited them.

Davis sniffed and sat back again, a wide smile lifting his cheeks. "Didn't mention that, did he? Did he also forget to mention your soon-to-be mother-in-law and your fiancée's unborn child's grandparents? I'd start there if I were you, Waters." Captain Davis got up and walked to his door, resting his hand on the handle. "You're a smart man, Waters, but I'd suggest you get your facts straight before stampeding into my office again."

Mark stood to his full six-four and strutted past the older man whom he'd always looked up to, but now he realized how much shorter he was. He hoped Davis' reputation would at least stand tall through Mark's investigation. Because captain or not, Mark wouldn't cover for anyone who broke the law.

Even as a young boy, Mark's father had drilled into his head the importance of telling the truth, no matter what the situation. Even taking the video tape with Ashlyn on it from the night of Devin Burke's death had been one of the most difficult things he'd ever done, but it had been the right thing to do, and thankfully, Captain Davis had agreed.

Now there was no telling what would happen.

Davis opened the door for Mark, making it clear he'd terminated their conversation, as though his comment hadn't been a sufficient enough hint. "By the way, the city's not fronting overtime to solve the case of a murdered homeless man, so I'll see you on Monday morning."

Mark stopped in the doorway and turned to his superior. "I'm still in charge of the investigation then, I take it?" If Davis had wanted to, he could have kicked him off and put Townsend in command. Of course, he hadn't done that to begin with, so maybe he really hadn't known it'd been Buchanan.

"Yep. I have no concern that you'll find anything implicating me in the death of Wade Buchanan. Get some rest and do the job I know you're capable of, son."

Still ticked that Davis hadn't disclosed his relationship to the victim, Mark made one last remark before leaving, "We do need to discuss your relationship to the victim, Cap'n."

"Monday," Davis said with finality.

Mark glanced at his phone for the time, then made his slow way to his office on the other side of the station. Townsend was still gone, so maybe he was having some luck. Then again, on that side of town, he may have wandered into a seedy men's club looking for witnesses and decided to begin his Friday night festivities earlier than usual.

Mark mentally dissected the information he had, wondering how it all connected. He stopped cold. His father would have investigated the Buchanan case. He headed straight to the records room, hoping he was correct. Granted, if anything implicated Captain

The Library

Davis, more than likely the man would have had it shredded eons ago, but it was a start.

Mark signed out the file and then made a beeline to his car. He knew where to get any information that wasn't in the file: his mother's house. His father had kept duplicates of every file he'd ever worked, and since Mark worked at the same police station, he'd requested that his mother just store them in the basement.

Since it was still early, and he knew his mother would have barely taken time to eat breakfast, let alone lunch, he sent her a quick text to let her know he was on his way with her favorite. He wished she'd want something fancier, but a meal deal at Taco Bell was the extent of his mother's excursions.

His mother sent back a quick, "Yay!" She was the youngest fifty-year-old woman he knew. She'd only been in her early twenties when she'd met his father, but his father hadn't looked his age. Although Mark's father was almost two decades her senior, his parents had enjoyed everything together. It saddened Mark that his mother had been widowed so young, but she never seemed to want to date anyone after his father had been murdered. Of course, at the time, his death had been suspected to be a suicide, so the idea that he'd been unhappy in their marriage had always plagued her.

Mark had only found out in the last year that his father's death had actually been a murder. He shook the thoughts from his head. He hated thinking about the woman who'd killed his father, leaving his mother widowed. Hated that he had to find out the way he had. He'd meant to visit her in prison, but he still wasn't sure if he could face her.

After going through the drive-thru, Mark headed to his mother's house, a three-story English Tudor in one of the quietest and safest neighborhoods in Edenbury. On a third of an acre and more than forty-eight hundred square feet, the house was entirely too large for his mother. But she had a clear deed. And his father's military pension and social security were more than enough to sustain the lavish house she'd begged his father to buy when she was pregnant with Mark. Her rationale for wanting the house, she'd told Mark, was not because of its size, but because she thought it looked like something out of a fairy tale.

With its original woodwork and stained glass, Mark had to admit it did have a storybook appearance, but it wasn't a cottage by any means. Unlike most homes built in the early nineteen hundreds, his mother's house boasted bedrooms that were up to three hundred square feet. The den that she'd turned into her home office was twenty-foot long by twenty-foot wide and looked out over a redwood deck surrounded by lush green landscaping.

Mark parked his police cruiser outside the three-car garage and climbed the outside steps that led to the kitchen. He knocked to let her know he was there, but then used his key so she wouldn't have to get up, even though he knew she would anyway. After she did one more thing on her computer, that is.

The temperature in the house still felt comfortable, but in the next few months, the kitchen and den would be the only warm rooms by way of small furnaces.

Mark stepped off the rustic tile in the kitchen onto gleaming hardwood floors in the hallway. His mother had always kept them beautiful. He knocked on the wood frame that bordered the entrance to his mother's in-home office and then shook the Taco Bell bag. "Lunchtime, Mom."

Cheryl Lynn, as his father had always called her, looked up from behind her laptop and flashed him a smile, but then quickly started typing again. "Hang on a second, sweetheart. Let me just finish this tweet."

She spoke her typed words aloud as she attempted

to fit everything she wanted to say into the allowed character count. He'd created a monster when he introduced her to the online world. Not only did his mother spend all day promoting her business, she now spent hours socializing with people around the world about whatever caught her fancy.

At least he didn't have to worry about her being lonely. Rarely did he come by the house and not find her chatting away — and laughing — which made him feel great, so he was happy with the monster he'd created.

His mother smacked down the cover on the laptop and got up from behind her desk. Mark closed the distance and allowed her to wrap her arms around him first and then he enfolded her completely in a tight embrace.

Cheryl Lynn leaned back and stared up at him from her five-four, one-hundred-and-thirty-pound frame. "I have the best son in the world. Thank you, Mark." She took the bag from his hand and peered inside. "Perfect. Let's go out on the deck. It's too gorgeous to stay inside." She peeked up at him again. "Are you sure you aren't still growing?"

Mark squeezed his arm around her shoulders. "No, Mom. I think you're getting shorter." He laughed.

She laughed too, but then grimaced. "That's probably true. Where're Ash and my grandbaby?"

Mark loved that about his mother. She knew the baby wasn't his, but she'd never asked questions and had already accepted Ashlyn and her son as her family.

He pulled out a chair for his mother. "Ashlyn went to Erie to spend a few days at her grandmother's place. You know how she loves the property there."

"I do. She's always telling me as soon as she has the baby she wants to tackle my overgrown forest." His mother narrowed her eyes. "Isn't her mother living there now, though?"

Mark pulled in a deep breath, appreciating the scent of jasmine, but then let it out with a sigh. Evidently, Ashlyn and his mother had spoken more than he knew. "Yeah. I hate her being gone, but I guess it's a good thing. From what I understand, they made a breakthrough in their relationship."

His mother patted his hand. "That's good, Mark. I can see that her being away is causing you stress, but don't give Ashlyn a hard time. I'd tell you to stop worrying, but that would never happen. So instead, I'm going to tell you to give Ashlyn her space. She's been through a lot, but she loves you."

"I know, Mom. Thank you. I'm trying."

"You've always carried the world on your shoulders, Mark, but Ashlyn's a smart, independent woman. Be a strong shoulder for her, but don't smother her."

Mark raised his hands. "Have I done something that I should know about?"

"No, but I know you. You're just like your father."

"Is that such a bad thing?"

"Not at all, sweetheart. You possess all the wonderful qualities your father had and even more."

Mark cocked his head. "Such as?"

"You talk," his mother responded immediately. "Your father held everything inside and tried to handle all situations on his own. Maybe if he'd told someone what he suspected, he'd still be alive."

Mark reached for his mother's hand. "I'm sorry, Mom."

She smiled. "See ... What do you have to be sorry for? You were a child."

Mark chuckled. "I don't know. I'm just sorry that you've been alone for so long."

She unwrapped her burrito, squeezed two packets of sauce inside, then deftly wrapped it again. "I'm not alone, Mark. I happen to have the best son in the world."

He smiled. "Thank you, Mom."

"Thank you for lunch." She took a bite and then gazed out at her yard.

Mark decided to wait until after lunch to bring up looking at his father's files. It was too nice sitting quietly with his mother. Something he needed to do more often.

CHAPTER 14

Once again, Mark found himself in the library. He blindly lumbered his way up the stairs, using his hands to guide him until his eyes adjusted. At the end of the same aisle where he'd spoken to Jay the previous day, a long table held what resembled a panel of judges, or maybe it was a line-up of suspects. The room was dark and misty, but he recognized each of the four faces. Mrs. Davis; Captain Davis; his soon-to-be mother-in-law, Laura Allan; and Gregory Burke all sat behind the rectangular table.

Each of the persons involved in his case had a hardback book on the desk in front of them. Because of the tattered and worn condition of the novels — the spines barely held together — Mark couldn't make out any of the titles.

"Do you know who's responsible, Mark?" Jay's cool breath saturated the tiny hairs on the back of his neck, sending a shiver down his spine. Her slender hands moved down his arms, lifting them. He froze, not sure what she wanted or what secrets she possessed.

Why was he dreaming about Jay again? He realized he was dreaming. Knew these four people hadn't just positioned themselves in front of him, offering to confess their connections to the deceased.

"What are you trying to tell me, Jay? How are you involved?"

"I'm afraid," she whispered.

Mark turned around, his immediate reaction to protect the innocent. He'd always defended others; even in school he'd protected smaller students from bullies. "Why are you afraid?"

Jay's golden eyes glistened with unshed tears. "Because you won't believe me."

Mark stepped forward to comfort Jay, but then a loud bang behind him shook the books on the surrounding shelves. He wheeled to see Laura Allan banging her gavel against the book in front of her. "I told Ashlyn you were no good for her."

"But I —"

Davis slammed his gavel next, cutting off Mark's defense. "You're a lousy detective, Waters. Why are you wasting time with a librarian instead of chasing down real leads?"

"I'm not with Jay —"

Mrs. Davis whacked down her gavel directly after her husband's remark. "Have you found out who killed that old man, Markey? Why are you wasting your time talking to *her*?"

His anger brewing, he started toward the group, wondering what they were accusing him of, when the fourth person stood up.

Gregory Burke didn't use a gavel; instead, he hammered his fist into the book in front of him. "The Pennsylvania State Police Commissioner is a friend of my father's. I'll have you fired for hiding evidence in my son's case. And I'll make sure I get full custody of my grandson and make Ashlyn suffer."

"I didn't conceal evidence," Mark snapped. "This isn't about Devin. A man was murdered."

"No one cares about a homeless man, Mark," Jay whispered in his ear. "You are his only chance." She moved her hands to his chest, nudging him gently. "Help me."

The Library

Jay's cold lips touched his neck and Mark bolted upright.

His calico darted off the bed in response. Mark's heart raced in his chest. "Oh, my God, kitty, you scared the death out of me. What makes you think I want your cold, wet nose on me first thing in the morning?"

She jumped back on the bed, obviously realizing he wasn't going to kill her today, and rolled over on her back, purring. He gave her exactly two seconds of scratching between the ears. Any more than a couple of seconds and he'd overstimulate her, and she'd bite him. A lesson he'd learned about calicoes. *Women too*, he mused. It seemed there had to be a perfect balance between protecting and controlling. Having an easy-going disposition versus being a total pushover.

Right now he felt as if everyone was pushing him in a different direction, and he didn't care for it one bit. But the accusations in his dream were from his subconscious. No one had entered his dream and inserted those allegations.

He'd been feeling all of them on his own, even the charges that had no foundation. He had no desire for Jay other than what information she could offer him. He'd given Captain Davis all the information on Devin

Burke's demise via train and had let him decide whether to pursue the case.

But he did feel like a lousy detective at the moment, and he really missed Ashlyn. He didn't want her to go through with speaking to the Gregory Burke alone, and if he allowed her, then he wouldn't be good enough for her.

It was Saturday, and the captain had made it clear that the city wouldn't be paying overtime to investigate a homeless man's death. But since Laura Allan's name had popped up twice, he could sift through that information and see Ashlyn at the same time.

If Laura wasn't okay with him being there, he'd get a hotel room. Ashlyn had accepted his proposal and engagement ring, so he felt as though he should have some input in her life. And if he were being honest with himself at least, he just wanted to see her. Ached for her. He'd been keeping himself busy at work, but no way would he be able to go all weekend without holding her.

It was early, he knew, but she woke up at the crack of dawn most days now that she'd quit bartending. He pressed her number on his phone, knowing he should have just shown up.

"Hey, baby," her scratchy morning voice answered

the phone, warming his insides that she wasn't upset that he'd woken her.

"Hi, sweetness. Do you have any plans today?"

"Uh-uh. I'm exhausted, so I thought I'd just rest today."

Mark pulled the phone away from his ear and glanced at the time. If he left right now, he'd be there by ten a.m. "Okay. Sorry for waking you up. Go back to sleep. I'll call you at ten."

"I don't mind you waking me up, but yeah, that'd be better. I'm exhausted. Love you. Talk to you then."

He smiled. "I love you too. Get some rest."

That was easy. By the sound of it, even if she decided to go out, she wouldn't get out and about before noon, so he had plenty of time. In fact, he could even bring her breakfast.

Mark grabbed his gym bag from underneath the bed and stuffed it with two days' worth of clothes. He took a lightning-fast shower, skipped shaving and brewing coffee again, and was on the road within ten minutes.

After a quick stop at Mickey D's, he headed north. The easiest route was to drive to New York and then head over to Erie via I-86. It'd be a long day, but it'd be worth it.

At ten fifteen, he pulled through another

McDonald's drive-thru and ordered two bacon, egg, and cheese McGriddles and two large lattes. He knew Ashlyn's OB doctor wouldn't approve, but Ashlyn would be happy. No woman would turn away a man bearing a peace offering of a McDonald's breakfast sandwich and coffee. Not that they needed to make peace — their problems weren't with each other — but he figured it couldn't hurt.

As he turned onto her mother's street, he made the call he'd promised Ashlyn.

"Right on time," she said when she answered.

He could almost hear the smile in her voice, and he felt his mouth turn up in response to the fact that he'd be seeing that beautiful smile in a few seconds.

"Of course. Aren't I always?"

"Yes. You have good timing too," Ashlyn offered. "I just finished drying my mop of hair."

"Ahh ... too bad. I like it when it's damp."

Ashlyn didn't respond. She was as sharp as they came. The front door swung open, and Ashlyn peeked out, looking as fresh and cute as ever in her Pink sweatpants and long sweatshirt. She refused to wear maternity clothes, which he'd been quite okay with, since most of the outfits looked downright silly. Mark couldn't imagine Ashlyn wearing a shirt with *Baby on*

Board stitched across the front. Nope. Workout clothes were much more stylish in her opinion, and he had to agree with her assertion.

A large smile spread across her cheeks, but she didn't move from the stoop, which he understood. Climbing stairs, even a few, was one of her least favorite things to do nowadays.

Mark left his overnight bag, but grabbed the food and coffee and jumped down from his truck. "I brought breakfast."

Ashlyn planted her hands on her hips. "Oh, a coffee offering. Smart man."

Mark quickly strode up the driveway and took the steps of the front porch two at a time. He set the coffee cups and bag down on the front swing, then closed the distance between them. His hands went to her long hair immediately, which was still a little damp. "God, I missed you." He sealed his lips to hers and pulled her closer.

Ashlyn moved her hands up his chest and around his neck, retracting her lips just slightly. "I missed you too."

Moving his hands down her back, he pulled her close again. He nudged her lips open with his, his tongue tasting her cinnamon toothpaste. Thankfully, he'd just popped in a Tic-Tac as he pulled into her neighborhood. He explored her mouth, feeling as if he'd missed kissing her for months, not days.

A soft sigh escaped her throat, and he reveled in it. It was clearly a sigh of contentment. She'd missed him too. Mark pulled back and looked at her. "I really, really missed you. I think I forgot how lonely I was before we met." He smiled as he thought about his words. "Do you realize this is the first time we've been apart in six months? You've always been at my place ... or I've been at yours."

Ashlyn laughed. "Yeah, kind of silly, huh? Paying for two apartments, I mean."

Mark's eyes widened. "Umm ... are you saying ..."

Ashlyn raised her fingers to his lips. "Let's eat, Mark. We can talk about *stuff* when I'm not half-dressed standing on the front stoop."

He smiled. "I happen to like you half-dressed." He reached for her other hand, happy that his ring was on her left hand. So she had to have told her mother. That was good. He bent down in front of her and touched her round belly. "Hey, baby. Have you missed me too?"

"Ooh!" Ashlyn jumped, then laughed again. "I think he did."

Mark moved his hands to where she directed him,

delighting at the life inside. "Wow. You think he recognized my voice?"

Ashlyn reached for the coffee and opened the front door. "How could he not? Like you said, we've seen each other every day for six months, and you speak to him as if he's here."

Picking up his cup and the bag, he followed Ashlyn inside. "He is here. He can hear." Mark looked around the living area and into the kitchen. "Where's Laura?"

"Oh, she's at the gym. Had a Zoomba class, she said."

"Well, that's one thing I can say about your mother; she keeps herself in tiptop shape." He took the coffee cup from her and set it on the table along with his, then drew her toward him. "How long will she be gone?"

One side of Ashlyn's mouth curved up in one of his favorite smiles. "Aren't you hungry, Mark?"

"I'm famished." He dropped onto the sofa and pulled her down beside him.

"Look at me. I'm huge. I think I've gained ten pounds in the last few days."

Mark ran his hand over her stomach, pulling up her shirt and kissing her soft skin. "It's all right here. And I love every inch of you."

Ashlyn giggled but pulled her sweatshirt back over her tummy.

He frowned in response. "Okay," he said on a sigh. "I can wait. I came here to see you, not to attack you."

"I really am starving, though." Ashlyn laughed. "Of course, what else is new?"

Mark stood up, retrieved their food, and returned to the couch. He handed her the sandwich and then sat back against the arm of the couch, content just to watch her.

"This is so good ..." she moaned through the first bite.

Mark felt a rush of desire, wishing he were causing that reaction in her. He hadn't been thinking about making love to Ashlyn. But the moment she was in his arms, he wanted her so badly it was almost painful. It wasn't just a physical reaction; his entire body felt on fire. His soul longed to hold her, to never let her go.

No doubt, Ashlyn was the only woman he'd ever want again. Those stupid dreams he'd been having weren't about wanting another woman. He had no interest in Jay; he only wanted her to confess what she knew.

As he thought back to the dream, he realized she was trying to show him something. Tell him a secret

The Library

he wouldn't believe, she'd said. Her hands had been trying to direct him. The aisle in the library. The others were trying to stop him, but she'd wanted to show him something there.

Mark shook the thoughts from his head. Captain Davis was right. Nothing would change in the next two days. He couldn't bring back the dead. And whatever secrets the library held, they'd be there on Monday. But would Jay? Would whomever or whatever she was scared of try to silence her?

CHAPTER 15

Ashlyn changed into clothes that were more suitable than the worn-out sweatpants and sweatshirts she'd donned all week — actually, the last two months. Mark was probably tired of seeing her in them. As soon as she had her baby, she'd burn them and lay them to rest.

He would love the babydoll tank she found in a Victoria's Secret catalog, she was certain. It worked well over leggings as makeshift maternity wear. Yeah, she looked pregnant, but it was clear she *was* pregnant. She hated when people looked at her and hem hawed around about the question. Did they honestly think she'd just suddenly gained weight all in her belly? It'd take a lot of six packs to do that.

Mark never made her feel huge, though. For some

reason, he seemed just as attracted to her as he had been at the beginning of their relationship ... before she'd started showing.

"Ash," Mark said as he knocked on the door. "Your phone is ringing. Unknown caller. Want me to answer?"

She couldn't help but smile. Her ex would have just answered it, or questioned why an unknown caller was calling her. "No, but you can come in now." As jealous as Devin had always been, it made no sense that he would have broken up with her so quickly and then insisted she have an abortion. Thank goodness Mark wasn't anything like him.

Mark inched open the door, holding her phone out as if he felt embarrassed for touching it. "I wasn't sure if it was important." He stepped closer. "Mmm ... I like." He ran his fingers over the lace that edged the low-cut scooped collar, which highlighted her greatly increased bust size. "When did you get this?"

"I ordered it and it arrived the day I left. I was saving it for you, and here you are." She smiled. "Why exactly did you drive five hours?"

Mark shoved her phone in the front pocket of his faded blue jeans and wrapped his arms around her.

"The same reason I brought your phone upstairs. I miss you."

"And you wanted to see my bedroom ..." Ashlyn trailed off.

Mark glanced around the room. "We couldn't," he whispered. "What if your great-grandmother saw us?"

"Do you really think —"

Mark placed his fingers over her lips. "Believe what you want. I know what I saw." He pressed his lips against hers and backed her up to the bed. Scooping her up in his arms, he placed her on the bedspread. "Maybe we can fool around for a little bit, though." He kissed her neck and nibbled his way up to her ear as he hovered over her. "I really did miss you."

Ashlyn giggled as his warm breath caressed her neck. "I missed you too, Mark." She buried her hands beneath his T-shirt, tracing every muscle in his back, then ran her fingers down his lats, delighting in the chilly bumps on his skin. Moving to his chest, she lifted the front of his shirt until, catching the hint, he pulled it over his head. Taking advantage of the situation, Ashlyn traced his chest, reveling in the sculpted lean muscle.

He was the most remarkable specimen of a man. Tall, but graceful. Muscular, but not bulging. Before she'd gotten too large, they'd started doing CrossFit together. The combination of cardio and strength training had assisted her to get in the best shape of her life, before she started showing, that is.

Mark looked as yummy as ever; he'd obviously continued training without her. She'd missed him too in the last few days, and her body reacted to his closeness in a way she'd never felt. She wasn't sure if it was the hormones or the fact that she hadn't seen him in a few days, but she was ready to rip off his clothes. Well, she'd already gotten rid of his shirt.

Mark lowered himself beside her and pulled her closer. "So, where will you take me today?"

Caught off guard, Ashlyn leaned back. "What do you mean?"

"Well, this is your stomping grounds. I'd like you to show me where your grandparents took you as a child. Or where you snuck off to escape your mother as a teenager."

"Oh. I was going to go home today. I really need to see the Burkes."

Mark sealed his lips in a line and then seeming to relax, he curled his hand behind her neck. "We'll do that tomorrow. I'll drive you home so you don't have to take the train, and then we'll go together."

"But I thought you said —"

"Forget what I said. What kind of husband would I make if I let you do one of the hardest things you've ever had to do on your own?"

Ashlyn felt the tears well up in her eyes and moved against Mark's chest so he wouldn't see them and think she was upset. "Thank you, Mark. That means a lot to me."

He gathered her closer, enveloping her with his embrace, and as always, she felt safe. "I love you, Ashlyn. As I said, I love all of you and will stand by you through everything you have to endure, good and bad."

Her heart thumped out a rhythm in response. She believed him and wanted him so much — forever. "So, when would you like to get married?"

Mark pulled back unexpectedly. "Really?" His green eyes seemed to sparkle like water she'd seen in pictures of the Mediterranean. He blinked to clear them, though. As sensitive as he was, he was strong. She'd never seen him tear up even remotely, and yet, her comment had caused that momentary reaction. It touched her soul more than any words he could ever utter.

She felt her own eyes fill again, but didn't try to

restrain them this time. "Yes, really. I told you I'd marry you. I was just worried. But I can see you really mean it when you say you want me and all my baggage too."

Mark frowned. "I never said you had baggage."

"Oh, but I'm saying it." She snuggled against his chest and he kissed the top of her head. "Thank you for wanting all of me."

He moved his hands to her face. "I'd like to get married right away, before the baby comes. Privately. And then we can have a huge wedding — whenever you want — so you can wear a designer dress and sip champagne."

Ashlyn smiled and felt her cheeks warm. "And wear lingerie on our honeymoon."

"That too," Mark said, grinning. "But I like this too." He traced the lace again. "I like these too."

"I'm sure you do. Maybe they'll stay around a while."

Mark lowered his head to her décolletage — as Mémé would have called it — and pulled the stretchy material down a fraction to expose the softer skin of her chest. His lips barely made contact when she heard the front door.

Ashlyn backed away from Mark as though she were

sixteen. Mark jumped out of the bed on the opposite side, his cheeks flushing instantly.

Smoothing her top and checking in the mirror that she was sufficiently covered, Ashlyn smiled at Mark's embarrassment. "Damn. Mom has impeccable timing."

"Yeah." He walked around to her side of the bed and scooped up her hand. "Let's go."

She couldn't help the burst of laughter. She was twenty-three and Mark was twenty-nine, and yet, they obviously both felt like high school students who'd been caught by their parents.

They strolled down the stairs together, startling her mother.

Laura glanced up the stairs, her eyes wide. "Mark. What a surprise. Ashlyn didn't tell me you were coming."

"I just woke up this morning and decided I couldn't go through the weekend without seeing both my babies."

Laura lifted her brow at his comment, but nodded as if she decided instantly that it was the correct response. "Well, I'm glad you're here, young man. Would you be a dear and get the rest of the groceries?"

"Gladly." Mark kissed Ashlyn on the cheek and

bounced down the rest of the steps and out the front door.

"He's such a nice young gentleman," Laura said. "And so handsome. I believe he is the best-looking man you've ever dated, Ashlyn."

Not sure if that was a compliment to Mark or an insult to her, Ashlyn pursed her lips to bite back a response. Her mother had a way with words. "Thank you," she finally said, deciding that ignoring her mother's word play was the best plan of action.

At least it wasn't a knock against Mark. The remark had only offended her. It was true, of course, but it wasn't as though she'd dated ugly men. She'd just never been particularly concerned with looks. As long as a man was pleasant-looking enough, and more importantly, a self-made businessman, she'd never cared too much about what they looked like.

Devin, of course, was attractive, but had turned out to be ugly inside. With Mark, neither looks nor money had caught her attention; it was his inner strength. Mark had an air of confidence about him that was neither haughty nor arrogant. He just had a self-assured attitude from the moment he'd asked her to dance. Without a doubt, she'd fallen in love with him on the first evening.

He was strong and wanted to shield her from all the evils in the world. From the first night they'd met, he'd wanted to protect her. It was a bonus that he was so incredibly handsome, and something she'd learned after falling for him, a self-made man. No, he didn't have the ridiculous amount of money that the Burkes had, but he did more than well. And when they finally combined households, they'd be quite comfortable.

Really, she wouldn't even have to work, but her company had already agreed to let her work out of the home until she felt comfortable introducing her child to social interactions, which from all she read, seemed to be about a year.

Mark came through the front door, plastic bags lined up both arms, and a case of soda tucked under one arm.

"Mom, I told you I was leaving this weekend," Ashlyn said. "That looks like enough groceries for a family of four for a week."

Laura waved her hand. "I can freeze what we don't eat." She took the twelve pack of soda from Mark and led the way to the kitchen. "Besides, I'm glad I did. I'm sure Mark has a healthy appetite."

Mark glanced over his shoulder at Ashlyn and grinned. "I do, Ms. Allan."

The Library

Ashlyn followed the two strangers into the kitchen and scooted onto a barstool at the counter. She watched as her mother and fiancé interacted civilly for the first time.

Mark was one of the few men that Ashlyn had ever introduced to her mother that she'd actually liked. Her mother had practically swooned the first time she met Mark; that is until Ashlyn explained that he was a police detective she met during the most traumatic situation in her life.

"Call me Laura," her mother continued. "We're practically related. No need to be so formal."

Ashlyn shook her head behind her mother's back, wondering where this sudden motherly attitude had come from.

Mark made his way over to the counter and kissed Ashlyn on the cheek. Obviously noticing her utter shock, he winked as he answered her mother, "Thanks, Laura. Is there anything else you need help with?"

"Nope. You kids go ahead and have a great day. But I'd like you home by seven for dinner."

This time Ashlyn couldn't contain the surprise. A chuckle slipped out of her mouth, causing her mother to turn toward her.

"What?" Laura asked, placing her hands on her hips in the most motherly fashion Ashlyn had ever seen. Was it possible that she and her mother could actually have a mother-daughter relationship?

"Nothing," Ashlyn said. "Seven o'clock is perfect. What are you making?"

"Spaghetti okay?" her mother asked.

"Perfect," Ashlyn said, and it was. Even her mother couldn't mess up spaghetti, and Mark loved anything with pasta. "All right then, Mom. I'm going to take Mark to Harbor View Golf."

Laura waved them off and Ashlyn took Mark's hand and led him to the door.

"Golf?" He raised his hands in confusion. "I'm terrible at golf."

Ashlyn grinned as Mark opened the door for her and helped her into his truck. She could manage of course, but being eight months pregnant, it wasn't a good idea to pull anything. "Don't worry. I'll teach you."

Mark closed her inside and made his way to the driver's side. He turned the key, backed out of the driveway, but then stopped at the exit before leaving the subdivision. "Since when do you play golf?"

"Would you trust me, silly?"

The Library

Mark followed directions, and within ten minutes, Ashlyn directed him down State Street toward Harbor View. It was hard to spot the well-hidden tiny golf course, but that was the beauty.

Mark laughed. "Got it! You sure you're up for this? I'm a champion at putt-putt."

"You just wait. This golf course is different from others. A little thing called *Mischief Spinners* evens up the odds since your girlfriend is a walking whale."

"Fiancée," he corrected her. "And you're not a whale." Mark parked the truck and rushed around to her side, allowing her to slide into his arms and gently setting her down. "This place looks like fun."

"Oh, it is! And wait'll you see the view. I want to take you to Presque Isle State Park next. You can see it from inside the course, though."

Mark escorted Ashlyn into the tiny building and paid for their two rounds of 18-hole miniature golf. He handed her a club with a pink handle and toted his red-handled club as though he were a pro golfer. He made a few practice swings. "Of course it's too short. I don't think they make putt-putt clubs for six-four men."

She laughed. "I'm sure they do; they probably just don't get a lot of giants here."

He grinned and motioned for Ashlyn to go ahead with their first challenge. "Ladies first."

Ashlyn spun the Mischief Spinner. "Blind Putt. Cool! That's an easy one." She dropped her ball, closed her eyes, and raised her club to swing.

"Wait a second." Mark interrupted her mid-stroke. "How will I know if you close your eyes?" He stepped up behind her and placed his hands over her eyes. He didn't touch her anywhere else, but for some reason, a blast of heat erupted inside her body. The need to feel his touch had parts of her anatomy pulsing with anticipation.

She ignored her body's reaction to his touch, doing her best to squash the raging desire that felt as though it might burn right through her skin. Hoping Mark didn't feel the warmth of the schoolgirl flush she felt work its way across her cheeks, she lowered her club in search of her ball.

Ashlyn blindly touched her ball with the club, and making sure she didn't miss, she just barely pulled back and tapped it. As soon as Mark removed his hands, she opened her eyes and watched as the ball traveled up the hump, around the bend, bounced off the border, and rolled right into the hole. "Yay!" she screamed. "I've never made a hole-in-one."

The Library

"Hmm ... sure." Mark stepped up and spun the wheel. "Extra Obstacle," he said, laughing. "Great. I get to putt around a whale."

"Hey!" Ashlyn pouted, but stepped into his path, doing her best to take up as much room as she could.

Mark stepped forward and kissed her. "I'm just kidding, baby. You're my whale, and I'd love you no matter how big you got."

Ashlyn pulled her foot in just slightly as Mark swung. The ball went right between her legs, over the hump, banked off the side, and rolled within an inch of the hole.

Her sophisticated, always prim and proper husband-to-be proceeded to jump up and down, attempting to make an earthquake she guessed so the ball would roll in. When nothing worked, he tapped it, and she scratched a number *two* on the sheet next to her *one*.

Ashlyn spun and then quickly made her shot, since her *Runaway Ball* command would come into play after Mark made his shot.

Mark made his spin and then frowned. "Hands On." He laughed. "It would have been fun if you'd gotten that one."

"I'd have to pass on that prompt. At eight months

237

pregnant, I'm not getting on my hands and knees for anyone."

Mark raised a brow. "How about a kiss for good luck then?"

Ashlyn obliged with a peck, but Mark pulled her back for more. He glanced around after a second, making certain the foliage shielded them, she guessed, and wrapped his arms around her and took her mouth again. His kiss felt so good that she decided maybe putt-putt wasn't such a good idea. She'd rather just cuddle up the rest of the afternoon in his arms.

"Where's this park you mentioned?" Mark asked, evidently thinking the same thing as she was.

Ashlyn pointed toward the bay. "But we have to drive west to get there. It's about a fifteen-minute drive."

"Can we go now?"

Ashlyn nodded. "Yeah. Let's do that. But that means I win."

"I wouldn't have it any other way." He took her hand and led her back to the truck. They grabbed some towels and sunscreen at the Country Fair store and headed toward the park.

After discussions of manning a four-wheeled, pedal-driven cart, walks to one of the three lighthouses, and assurances of turtle and turkey sightings along one of the trails, Mark and Ashlyn decided that sitting on the beach, watching the waves and birds, would be the most enjoyable afternoon.

The weather was a perfect sixty-five and sunny, and she'd brought her jacket just in case it was windy. Ashlyn couldn't have ordered up a better day.

Mark assisted her to the towel and then sat down beside her, wrapping his arm around her shoulder. He pressed his lips against her neck. "You know," he whispered in her ear. "Before your mom interrupted us, we were discussing weddings and honeymoons ... and lingerie."

Ashlyn felt a deluge of arousal surge through her again. "I haven't forgotten." She leaned her body against his. "How soon?"

"I was thinking immediately," Mark responded without hesitation. "We could get a license on Monday and then plan to skip town next weekend." He tilted up her head. "Of course, that's just because I'd like to give you and our son my name. I still want to have the big wedding whenever you're ready."

Ashlyn peered up at him and gulped. "Okay."

"You said okay, but your eyes said, 'I'm scared,'"

Mark stated without a hint of condemnation, just concern.

"I'm not scared, Mark. I promise. I'm just concerned about what to do with the baby. I'm not sure about naming him."

Mark nodded, but she could see she'd hurt his feelings — again.

"Hear me out, Mark. This has nothing to do with us. This is about our son, and he will be your son. I just have to figure out the legalities and respectable thing to do. My mom mentioned another reason why she thought I should tell his grandparents. Mom didn't have grandparents. My grandmother grew up without a mother or father, just her grandparents, and then my mother had her mother and father — who were great — but she never had grandparents. And grandparents are fun."

Mark nodded. "I understand. I loved my grandparents, and I miss them. My father was forty when he had me, so they've been gone a long time. And my mother's parents died when she was young."

"I'm sorry. You never told me that. And your mother never told me. I feel terrible complaining about my mother when she lost hers."

Mark smiled and touched her face. "Don't feel sad.

The Library

My mother loves you. And she knows you don't complain needlessly and probably thinks along the lines, 'If I had a daughter, I'd ... '" He laughed at his imitation of his mother's voice. "She tells me all the time that I owe her granddaughters. So we better get started ..." He lowered his head to kiss her, and she cut him off before she forgot.

"Oh, wait. I found the coolest thing that I wanted to show you." Ashlyn reached into her shoulder bag and pulled out the old photograph she'd found in the cookbook. The more she thought about it, the more she was convinced. Even if the man in the photo hadn't killed her great-grandmother, she still had to have known him. Otherwise, why would his picture have been there? And the date matched. She handed the old black-and-white snapshot to Mark.

"Yeah, I heard your mother dated him. Weird, huh?"

Confused, Ashlyn cocked her head. "What do you mean? Dated whom?"

Mark pointed to the picture. "Gregory Burke. I heard your mother and he had dated each other all through high school."

"That's true, but what does that have to do with this photo? I just found it."

Mark laughed. "That's right. You've never seen him. Ashlyn, that's Gregory Burke. Your baby's grandfather."

Ashlyn shook her head as tears welled up in her eyes as the pieces of the puzzle clicked together. Her head swarmed with confusion, the blood pumping so fast, she felt she might pass out. As her blood pressure rose, Mark's face blurred before her eyes. She tried to fill her dry mouth with moisture so she could speak.

"Mark," she gasped, "look at the date." Goose bumps soared down her arms as a sudden chill swept through her body. "I think ... I think that's a picture of my great-grandfather."

Mark took the picture from her quivering hands and studied it, shaking his head repeatedly. "The date is wrong, Ash. This is Gregory Burke. I spoke to him several times."

"What if —" She gasped for air again. "What if he only looks like him? What if ... what if when Gregory Burke's grandfather found out he was dating my mother, I can't even think of how they'd be related, but he'd demanded they break it off? My mother said she and Gregory Burke were madly in love, planned to elope, but then he'd unexpectedly dropped her off in front of her house and never returned her phone calls. Then I dated Gregory's son ... Oh, my God! Why didn't I see the resemblance? Devin's eyes ..." Ashlyn tried to slow her breathing, but the panic had set in. "Devin loved me, Mark. He may have been mean to everyone else — tried to kill me even... But before then, he was crazy about me. He sat at the bar every single night waiting for me to get off work, even if we'd only have a few minutes together. Then out of nowhere he breaks up with me over the phone. When I called him a few weeks later and told him I was pregnant, he went ballistic. He even offered me a hundred thousand dollars to have an abortion. Just a few weeks before he'd broken up with me he'd been talking about kids and marriage." Ashlyn gulped in another mouthful of air. "Oh, no! We're related!"

CHAPTER 16

Mark rested his hands on both sides of Ashlyn's face. He understood her alarm, but it wasn't safe for her unborn child. "Baby, calm down. Breathe in through your nose, and hold it." She did as he told her. "Now breathe out through your nose. Then do it again."

She listened, but her tears continued to roll down her cheeks and over his hands.

"The relation is so far down the line it wouldn't cause any harm. Not that I'm condoning the practice, but in some places, first cousins still get married." He brushed his thumbs over her brows. "I know you're worried about the baby, but don't be. The stress you're feeling is far worse. It's only because close relatives can carry the same defective genes and of course the *eww* factor, but you'd be third cousins at best, right?"

Ashlyn gulped back the tears. "I don't know. I've been trying to compute it in my head. If it's true, then it means we have the same great grandparents. First cousins have the same grandparents. So, second cousins. *Eww* ..."

"Not exactly. If it's true, you only share one great grandparent on the Burke side. If it's true, the eldest Burke obviously married another woman after his affair with your great-grandmother, and had kids with the new woman."

"True, but —"

"I may be wrong, Ash. I'm sorry. That picture might not be of a Burke."

Ashlyn shook her head again. "No. The eyes ... it's there. I don't know why I didn't see it before. Maybe I didn't want to see it. When I talked to Mom last night, I asked her what happened. She said that when I'd told her about Devin, she realized again how strange her breakup with his father had been." Ashlyn dropped her head. "It makes so much sense now. Of course Gregory Burke's grandfather wouldn't have wanted to confess to him, but a first-cousin relationship is rather close, even if you're only half-cousins. I guess he wanted to keep my family as far away as possible."

Mark jumped to his feet and held out his hand to her. "Let's go. You won't be able to relax the rest of the day anyway. We need to speak with your mother tonight — and then Gregory Burke tomorrow."

The ride back to the house was quiet except for the sniffles from Ashlyn's side of the cab. Why hadn't he thought before blurting out Gregory Burke's name?

He pulled into the driveway and parked next to Laura's Benz, then raced around the front of the truck. He was at Ashlyn's door within a couple of seconds to help her down. He should have taken the time and called her so he could have come in her Jetta.

Impulsive. As sensible as he was most of the time, he could also be irresponsible. Especially when it came to Ashlyn. He'd wanted so badly to please her — from the moment they'd met — that he tended to throw caution to the wind. From now on, he'd think before speaking and acting.

Ashlyn leaned against him as they walked up to the house.

Mark stopped just outside the door. "We don't have to do this tonight, Ash. What's done is done, and nothing can bring back your great-grandmother. If

The Library

Burke's family had anything to do with her death, it wasn't —" Mark stopped his own words as more pieces of his puzzle clicked. As Jay's remarks in the library came rushing back to him.

Gregory Burke was a person of interest in the death of Wade Buchanan, since they'd had a large business deal going before Buchanan had disappeared twenty-eight years ago. For that matter, Laura had dated Gregory, who ended up dating Buchanan's daughter. And then Captain Davis had dated Buchanan's daughter before Gregory, and had been the first on the scene according to the report Mark's father had written twenty-eight years ago. Not to mention Mrs. Davis had fought the developers and the city to keep the deal between the Burkes and Buchanan from going down.

"What happened, Mark?"

Mark shook his head and sat down on the swing to clear his thoughts. "This is a damn soap opera, Ash."

"What is?"

"A lot of missing pieces have just come together in this murder case I'm working. Only problem is that they are all so closely related it's hard to see which piece fits where."

"What does this have to do with the situation we're in right now? What did you just think of?"

Mark ran his hands through his hair. "I'm not sure. Wade Buchanan, the homeless man who was murdered behind the library that I told you about ..." She nodded for him to continue. "He was in a business deal with Burke and the city for the library's property. It seems Buchanan owned parcels of land on both sides that had just been cheap strip malls. The library has several buildings which sit on several acres of land." Mark sat back against the backrest of the swing and looked up at the overhang. "Let me just work this all out aloud. Your mom dated Gregory Burke through high school. Captain Davis dated Wade Buchanan's daughter, Jessica. At the end of high school, Burke suddenly dumps your mother and dates Jessica. Captain Davis and your mom would have both been upset, as I'm sure they knew each other. Jessica had worked at the library, so she would have known Mrs. Davis." He stopped and thought about Jay's words, *Mrs. Davis would do anything to save her precious library.*

"I'm trying not to interrupt, Mark, but you just dazed off."

Mark patted her knee. "Hang on. Jessica would have had firsthand knowledge of the deal between her father and her fiancée Gregory Burke. She also would have known everything Mrs. Davis was doing to sabotage the deal." Mark leaned forward and rested his elbows on his knees. He remembered his father doing this exact same thing when he was working out a scene. "Could Mrs. Davis have found something on the Burkes?" He sat upright again. "Could she have discovered a connection between the Burke family and the death of your great-grandmother? Maybe she told Jessica, and Jessica confronted Gregory."

"Oh!" Ashlyn clamped her hand over her mouth. "You think Gregory Burke might have killed Jessica, and then killed her father?"

Mark nodded. But then shook his head. "It's a lot of conjecture, but there's definitely a lot of smoke in the vicinity. And where there's smoke —"

"Well, I can't have that family anywhere near my baby." Ashlyn pushed herself off the bench and paced across the porch. "Oh, my God. They're all murderers. Great-grandfather, father, and son — Well, Devin only attempted to murderer. He probably would have succeeded, too, if it weren't for my great-grandmother's ghost — or whatever happened six months ago at The Depot. Hell, I'm sure the grandfather must have been guilty of something too."

Mark walked over to her and took her in his arms. "Ash, again, I'm sorry. This is all conjecture —"

"There are a lot of suspicious holes, Mark." She dropped her head on his chest. "Will my baby be all right? Will he inherit these genes?"

Mark stroked the back of her head. "Nurture plays a major role in character, Ash. Your son won't be growing up in the Burke household."

"That's why I can't tell them. None of them."

The door opened and Laura stepped out. The woman's previous distaste for him appeared to have surged to the surface. "What's going on?"

"Nothing, Mom."

Laura Allan glared at Mark, her hazel eyes darkening by the second. "What did you say to her?"

"Mark didn't do anything, Mom. Something else ..." Ashlyn trailed off, obviously not wanting to get into the details with her mother yet.

"Oh, okay. Sorry, Mark," Laura apologized through her teeth, clearly doubting Ashlyn's defense of him.

He waved his hand. "No, no, I'm fine. It was an easy misunderstanding." Actually, he was quite pleased that Laura was attempting to come to the rescue of her daughter. She'd never defended her before, according to Ashlyn. Of course, he couldn't say that aloud.

"Can you give us a minute, Mom?"

"Sure, sweetheart. Dinner's ready, though, so don't be too long." Laura walked back inside, pulling the door closed behind her.

Ashlyn pulled in a deep breath. "What should I do, Mark? I've not asked you, as I wanted to handle everything on my own without dragging you into this mess. But now I don't know what to do."

Mark took her hand and led her back to the swing. "Let me talk to Gregory Burke alone. I'll get to the bottom of this without mentioning you. Our baby has nothing to do with this mess. And I agree; I don't want the Burkes anywhere near our son until we know the truth."

Ashlyn nodded. "What did I do to deserve you?"

He kissed her softly. "Ashlyn, I ask myself that same question every day. Only in reverse. You are a beautiful, smart, and wonderful woman. I honestly don't know what I did to deserve you."

She laughed. "Right. Mr. Perfect."

Mark couldn't help but laugh at that. "Not even close. Remember I have a couple skeletons in my closet too. My sister's in prison for murder. That's not something I'm proud of. And my personal life hasn't been so squeaky clean either. Thankfully, all my loose ends have moved away."

Ashlyn crinkled her nose. "Speaking of *loose* ends. Was Miss Beautiful Strawberry Blonde working with you this week?"

Ignoring her jealousy — which he knew was only because she was pregnant — he decided to go with a different approach and said, "Almost Mrs. Beautiful Strawberry Blonde is sitting right beside me. You have nothing to fear, baby. You've hooked me forever. I'm not going anywhere." He pulled her hand to his lips. "I woke up at five a.m. and drove five hours today just to kiss you. I've never done that for any woman."

Ashlyn leaned against his shoulder. "I guess we better get inside before Mom comes looking, or worse, burns dinner."

Mark stood up and again extended his hand to his bride-to-be. She accepted and stood up next to him, moving in closer for a kiss, he assumed. He lowered his head to kiss her, but she moved to the side.

She lifted herself up on her tippy toes and whispered in his ear, "My door will be unlocked tonight. I'll expect you exactly twenty minutes after I go to bed — to comfort me, of course."

Mark leaned back to see if she was teasing him, but

the fire in her chartreuse-colored eyes told him everything he needed to know.

"Yes, Ma'am." He gathered her into his arms and her lips parted in acquiesce. Mark wasted no time in tasting those soft and full lips that always tasted of cinnamon. Their tongues moved together as though in a slow and sensual dance.

Ashlyn worked her fingers into his hair, and he did his best to keep his hands from wandering. As much as he wanted to feel her skin beneath his fingertips, they were outside and the neighbors might see.

Mark released a groan as he realized they had to stop or he wouldn't be able to walk back inside the house. "So, what time is bedtime? I've been up since five, so I'm exhausted."

Ashlyn smiled. "Mom and I were up late again talking, so I'm guessing she'll crash right after dinner."

"Let's go eat," Mark said, taking her hand and pulling her into the house. As a cop, he was used to eating on the run. Tonight would be a sprint.

CHAPTER 17

The next day, Mark sat in front of a custom-made mahogany desk as he waited for Gregory Burke. It had surprised him that Burke was willing to see him on a Sunday, and with such short notice.

The only thing it took to get the man's attention was mentioning that he was investigating the murder of Wade Buchanan.

The door swung open and the tall man strutted behind his desk without bothering to shake Mark's hand. "We meet again." Burke pursed his lips and held up his arms, then dropped them onto the armrest of his mahogany-colored leather chair that matched his expensive desk. "Any news on my son's murder, Detective?"

"Devin's case has been closed, sir. I'm here about the death of Wade Buchanan. I understand you were business partners, and you were engaged to his daughter, Jessica Buchanan, who was found murdered along with her mother. Many of the people you know seem to die, Mr. Burke."

Gregory Burke leaned back in his plush leather chair. "So, Buck's dead?" he said, ignoring the rest of Mark's thinly veiled accusations.

Mark nodded. He saw no reason to speak as long as Burke was willing to supply the conversation. He'd only stated all that information, so he could watch Burke's reaction.

"How did Buck die?"

"Shot."

"Do you know who shot him?"

Mark scratched the back of his neck. "We haven't made an arrest yet, sir, if that's what you mean."

Burke removed his glasses. Taking a handkerchief from his pocket, he proceeded to breathe moisture onto the glasses and then wipe them off.

"That son of a bitch killed my fiancée," Burke said as nonchalantly as though he were talking about the weather.

"Tell me about that, Mr. Burke," Mark said. "What

makes you think Wade Buchanan killed his wife and daughter? What motive did he have?"

Burke shrugged. "I figure he had a mistress. When things started going sour with the deal, he ran."

Mark leaned forward. "But the deal didn't go through, right?"

Burke rested his hands in front of him, addressing Mark with a frown as though he were an employee who'd screwed up. "The deal wasn't completely over, but it was heading that way. So Buck cashed the first installment of the money we'd given him for his property — the night he murdered his family, I might add — knowing the deal wasn't final until the acquisition of the city property, and ran."

"But Wade Buchanan didn't run."

Burke cocked his head to the side. "What do you mean? He's been gone for twenty-eight years. Of course he ran."

Mark sat back in his chair, watching as Burke mirrored his actions. Either Burke was an incredibly good liar or he really didn't know that Wade Buchanan had disguised himself as a homeless man. Of course, that's not to say that Buchanan hadn't taken off and then come back recently. Maybe he'd owed debts to someone else and that person caught up with him behind the library. Captain Davis had mentioned that Wild Bill had a gambling problem and had many debts, too. Maybe Buchanan had owed him.

The information was public record, so Mark saw no need to hide the truth. Rather, he thought it'd be better to watch Burke's reaction. "Wade Buchanan was homeless. He'd been seen in the library, even made friends with one of the librarians and a few of the vagrants. So far I've traced his activities back six months."

"What about the cop?" Burke asked. "Jessica's ex-boyfriend. I never liked him. And he just so happened to be the first on scene."

"Mr. Burke, I came here to discuss Wade Buchanan's death, not his family's."

Burke bolted out of his chair. "Find out who killed Jay and you'll find out who killed her father."

A clammy wetness spread over Mark's skin. "What ... did ... you ... say?" His throat caught and the room seemed to drop in temperature about twenty degrees. Mark looked at his hands. They were pale white. He dropped his head between his knees and tried to ignore the blood pumping in his ears.

A distant voice, as though he were in a pool of water, asked if he was all right. Mark attempted to shake his head, but wasn't sure if he'd managed to move it. His head no longer felt attached to his body.

"Mark ..." Jay's voice came to him loud and clear. "It's okay, Mark. I told you that you wouldn't believe me."

Mark sat up slowly and the beautiful redhead was standing in front of him. He glanced about the room, but no one else was there. He was still in Burke's office. Was he dreaming again? Or had he finally lost his mind?

He reached out to touch Jay, but though she looked as real as Ashlyn, his hand moved right through her. Her image broke apart, as if he'd waved away steam from over a pot of boiling water. Her image reappeared next to him, causing his heart to thrash even harder. He *was* going insane. He had to snap himself out of this. But then again, maybe there was something else in his subconscious that he'd missed — or seen. Maybe he'd seen something in the library when he was a child.

Deciding that he should take advantage of his hallucination, he asked, "Who killed you, Jessica?"

She moved her head back and forth. "My friends call me Jay. You're my friend, right, Mark? You wouldn't hold a little thing like being a ghost against me, would you?"

The Library

Mark blinked his eyes, trying to dispel the image. "You're just a figment of my imagination, Jay. Or else Burke would still be here."

"You okay, Detective?" Gregory Burke spoke from behind him.

Mark whipped around and saw the older man carrying a can of Coke.

Burke handed Mark the aluminum can. "They say the syrup helps. You looked as though you were in shock. Never saw the blood leave someone's body the way it did yours. You looked like a ghost."

Mark choked on the soda and covered his mouth. He glanced around the room for Jay, but of course, she wasn't there. He really was going insane — or maybe he'd already gone insane, and just didn't know it yet.

"Are you diabetic? Do you need a candy bar or something?"

Mark waved his hand. "I'm fine. I didn't eat this morning, so my blood sugar must be low." He sat back in the chair and took a deep breath, still unable to keep his gaze from darting around the room. Burke probably thought he'd smoked crack before coming here. He was acting paranoid.

Burke sat down behind his desk again, his mood

friendlier. *Maybe I should have a panic attack in front of all suspects*, Mark mused.

"Where were we?" Burke asked.

Mark squeezed the back of his neck, not really wanting to know the truth, but hoping he was wrong. If Jay was currently a librarian, and it was just a coincidence that Burke had called his fiancée Jay, it would mean he was just suffering from delusions, not seeing ghosts. "You mentioned finding out who murdered Jay. Who is Jay?"

"Jay was my fiancée. Her name was Jessica, but she always signed her notes with just a *J*, so everyone called her Jay."

Mark inhaled a breath, willing his heart to slow. "Do you happen to have a picture of her?"

"Sure." Burke got up and crossed the room to a bookshelf. He grazed his fingers across four leather-bound books. Selecting the one farthest to the right, he pulled it out and walked back to Mark. "I don't have any photos. Wife wouldn't have liked me keeping any, but I have my high school yearbooks. Jay was a grade behind me, so it's in black and white, though."

Burke flipped through a few pages and then stopped. He traced his fingers over the paper and then walked toward Mark, lowering the book and pointing to the image.

Mark's heart felt as though it would pound itself right out of his chest as he stared down at the beautiful young woman. She would have only been sixteen, but it was the same Jay he knew ... met ... whatever they'd call what they'd done. Connected, maybe?

Mark ran his hand across his mouth. Not sure where to go with this information, he decided to ask Burke a few more questions and then get out of there. He really needed to question Jay, he supposed. But she'd said that she didn't know who killed her. Only that it was one of four people.

"Do you know Laura Allan?" Mark asked.

For the first time, Gregory's countenance changed. His shoulders drooped and his mouth fell. The man appeared to have aged ten years before Mark's eyes. "Yes."

"You dated her, right?"

"Yes."

"Why did you break up?"

Gregory Burke looked up. A sheen of moisture covered his blue eyes. "Money."

"What do you mean? I thought your family was well off."

Burke sat back in his chair. "My grandfather and father threatened to cut me off if I didn't break up with her. But I didn't care. I loved Laura. I would have given up everything I had and everything that was coming to me for her. Prom night I posed the question, asked her if she'd still love me if it weren't for my family's wealth. She'd tried to play it off, but no matter how I asked, it was clear. She wouldn't want me if I was penniless." Burke blew out a long breath. "And I was right. After Jay died, and I'd refused to talk to anyone, including Laura, she went to Hollywood and married some big exec. The moment he retired, however, she was calling me, saying she didn't want to be with a *nobody*. I'd married my current wife by then, though. Laura even had the nerve to apologize about Jay's death even though she'd harassed her before she died."

"What kind of harassment?"

"Just phone calls and such. Even when she wasn't volunteering, Jay spent most of her time in the library working on school projects. So Laura would call the library. Evidently, Laura had shown up a few times too. I'm not really sure what she said; Jay never told me. Jay was a tough girl. Sweet as can be, but smart as a whip. She'd laughed it off, saying she knew exactly how to handle Laura. Insisted the next time she saw Laura she could guarantee that she wouldn't come around either of us ever again."

Mark could see that in Jay, even if she was a ghost. He laughed internally, but then realized how ridiculous it sounded that he thought he knew a ghost. He wondered if he could commit himself or if he'd have to get his mother or Ashlyn to have him committed. What could Jay have found that would have caused Laura to back off? Had Jay known about Laura's possible relation to Gregory Burke? Not wanting to feed Burke any of that information, though, Mark nodded for Burke to continue.

Burke shook his head. "I guess one time it'd become rather heated. I assume it was with Laura, as she was the only person who ever seemed to upset Jay. Jay never gave me specifics, but when I'd picked her up after work one night, she was shaking, asking me if I knew some woman."

Mark leaned forward.

"I don't remember why, but she wanted to know if my father or grandfather ever mentioned the woman's name to me."

"Do you remember the woman's name?" Mark asked.

Burke shook his head again, but then his lips moved

as though he were trying a few names. It looked as though he were mouthing the alphabet. Mark had done that.

"E, I think," he said. "Edie, maybe? Edna?"

Mark's stomach fell again. Jay had known about Edda. Mark didn't want to give Burke any names, but he was so close. "Edda?"

Burke slammed his hand against the desk. "That's it. Edda." Then he narrowed his eyes. "How did you know that?"

"Edda Barrett was Laura Allan's grandmother. She was murdered when she was nineteen."

CHAPTER 18

Gregory Burke looked up as his door swung open and an older gentleman, who had the same white-as-snow and thick-cropped hair and bright blue eyes as Gregory did, walked into his office without knocking.

Gregory Burke's father, Mark presumed. The hair and brows were distinctive; he'd recognized the same traits in Devin. Evidently, the male gene was dominant in the family. The thought sent a swell of fear through him. He'd never once had a concern about fathering Ashlyn's son. He'd looked forward to it actually. At twenty-nine, he'd started to feel the pull toward fatherhood. He'd hoped he wouldn't end up like his father and not have a child until he was forty-something.

What if Ashlyn's son looked, sounded, and acted as these men did, though? Would it bother him? He shook the thoughts from his head. At least Gregory had seemed genuinely in love with Laura. He could have been lying, of course. The family had obviously held some dark secrets for years.

"Gregory, what do you think you're doing?" the older man spit out. Literally. Mark leaned back, hoping not to catch any spraying spittle. "I've —"

The younger Burke held up a finger, cutting off his father's words mid-sentence. "Excuse me, Dad." Gregory turned back to Mark. "I'm confused. You think my fiancée was asking me about a woman my family might have known who was related to my ex-girlfriend. Why?"

"Excuse me, Detective Waters, is it?" Gregory's father wagged a finger at him. "Your father was Wilson Waters, right?"

Mark nodded.

"He was a fine detective. I knew him and the other fellas at the station. I just so happen to be good friends with the police commissioner. I don't think he'd take kindly to you badgering citizens in their home. If you have any more questions for my son, I suggest you go about it the proper way. I'll be contacting my attorney immediately."

Mark wasted no time. He stood to leave.

Gregory looked between his father and Mark. "What's going on? I don't have a problem answering a few questions. I haven't done anything."

The older man crossed his arms. "Doesn't matter."

Mark refused to look at the older Burke and turned his gaze back to Gregory. "I just had a few questions about a man that your family was involved with years ago who turned up dead a few days ago. Evidently your father would rather you not answer a few questions."

"Not without an attorney present," the elder Mr. Burke said, moving closer to his son's desk as though he were a sentry sent to protect the prince.

Mark tipped his head as if he wore a hat. He didn't dare ask a question once a suspect requested an attorney. Anything a person of interest in a case said from that point without their lawyer present could endanger getting an arrest warrant or conviction in court if it ever went that far. "Thank you for your time, Mr. Burke. I'll be in touch."

Mark showed himself to the door and headed back to Laura's house. It was hard to know if the info he had gathered would help or not. If Ashlyn's mother had known that the Burkes had connections to her grandmother's death, wouldn't she have said something years ago? After all, that would have made her an heir. That would have been one hell of a slap in the face to the man who'd dumped you for another woman.

But Laura had tried to get back together with Gregory after Jessica had been murdered. Two things in that scenario didn't fit. If Laura had known, and yet tried to get back together, it would have meant that she knew Gregory was her first cousin. And marrying a first cousin *was* illegal in Pennsylvania. If Laura had told Jessica about a Burke possibly murdering Edda, thinking Jessica would tell Gregory, that'd hurt Laura's case of Gregory ever coming back to her rather than help it.

Of course, when had Laura Allan ever been rational? Before today, that is. In the mere six months Mark had known her, he'd witnessed a spoiled, fame-seeking woman who wasn't even above using her daughter in order to accomplish her goals.

With nothing but time to fill during the long ride back to Ashlyn, his mind continued to wander. Then finally, without his consent, his thoughts traveled back to his *episode* in Gregory's office. It'd been so real, but then again, it hadn't. Jay's image had been as real as any human body until he tried to touch her; then her body had been ethereal.

He thought back to the few times he'd spoken to Jay at the library, how she'd backed away from him every time he stepped toward her. Her face had been so clear, so pale, almost fake-looking in its beauty, he realized.

As silly as he felt, he decided to try to connect with her, even if she was a ghost. "Jay, can you hear me?"

Nothing.

Since he was the most stubborn man, according to his mother and Ashlyn, and admittedly, he knew it too, he spent the entirety of the trip pleading with Jay to talk to him, even though he didn't believe in ghosts.

Still nothing.

He pulled onto Ashlyn's driveway and dragged himself up the stoop. Almost fifteen hours of driving in just a little over twenty-four hours and spending hours in the car attempting to make contact with a ghost, who suddenly didn't want to connect, was tiring.

Under normal circumstances, the captain would've cussed him out for calling in sick during an investigation, but oddly enough, Mark was certain he wouldn't complain too much this time. Mark decided that he'd stay at Laura's another night, making sure he questioned her this time, and then tomorrow, he and Ashlyn would drive home together.

The front door to the house opened before he touched it. Ashlyn's eyes were expectant, but evidently reading the distress in his, her demeanor fell quickly. "Is everything okay? What did you find out? Do they know?" She threw several questions at him all at once.

Noticing that Laura's car was in the driveway, Mark took Ashlyn's hand and led her down the steps to his truck without speaking. He closed her in the passenger side and then hopped up into the cab beside her.

Why was he so tired? He lowered his head to the steering wheel, feeling as though he could sleep right there.

"You okay?" she asked as she scooted next to him.

Unable to speak, he shook his head.

"Baby, what's wrong?" She nudged his head up from the steering wheel. "What did Gregory Burke say? Did he threaten you?"

Mark couldn't help the spurt of laughter that burst out of his mouth at the thought of Ashlyn protecting him from the big, bad Burkes. It looked as though she were ready to take them on singlehandedly. Unfortunately, the humor was short-lived.

He threw his head against the headrest and exhaled a long sigh. "I think I'm going mad, Ashlyn."

"What do you mean?"

"I know you don't believe what I saw, and I don't understand why it's clearer to me, but I know what I saw." He shook his head. "I never told you the rest of it because I didn't want you to think I was crazy. But even before I saw your great-grandmother's image, the night I investigated the scene I heard someone whispering, and then I felt something clamp down on my shoulder. I don't understand how or why, but I think I have a connection to ghosts."

"I don't understand, Mark. Why are you talking about this now? That was six months ago. Why would you think I'd suddenly think you were crazy now?"

"Because Edda's ghost isn't the only one I've seen. I've been talking to a woman, Ashlyn. A twenty-two-year-old redhead who works at the library." Ashlyn's eyes narrowed. "Yeah, she's pretty, but you have nothing to fear. Not that you would anyway, but the woman I've been talking to the last couple of days is the ghost of a woman who was murdered twenty-eight years ago."

Ashlyn laughed, but then seeing his expression, covered her mouth. "You're serious?"

"Deadly — sorry, no pun intended." He dropped his head. "I don't know what this means."

"I don't think it means anything, Mark." She moved closer and rested her hand on his forearm. "Some people have the ability to sense things that others don't."

"Are you sure? Because I've been thinking maybe I need a rubber room."

Ashlyn restrained a laugh again.

"I'm glad you can laugh about this," he said. "How would you like not knowing whether someone is real or fake? I didn't know that she was a ghost until today when I reached out for her."

Ashlyn bolted upright and did the head-bobbing thing before she even started speaking. "And why were you reaching out for her?"

"Baby, would you please give the jealousy bit a rest? I swear to God, I have no desire for any other woman. I asked you — no, begged you to marry me. I've begged you to come home for days. Drove five flippin' hours to be with you, then drove another five hours to talk to Gregory Burke, and back to you again. Then I tell you I'm having conversations with a dead woman and you're wondering if I'm cheating on you —"

"I'm sorry," she jumped in before he could say anymore.

"It's okay. I just can't imagine why you'd even think for a second I'd want another woman, when I've spent every day of the last six months showing you how much I love and want you."

"I know ..." she whimpered. "Can I blame it on hormones and the body of a whale?"

He laughed. "You don't have the body of a whale. You look like a beautiful pregnant woman. So cut it out." He nudged up her chin so he could look her in the eyes. "Did you feel like a whale last night?"

"No," she said, blushing. "Not at all."

"All right then." He sighed. "Are you ready for the rest of my story?"

She nodded.

He proceeded to give her the play-by-play of the conversations with Jay from the first day at the library, the dreams, and then his almost nervous breakdown at the Burkes' residence.

"You know," he said through a laugh, "I should have known from the first day." Ashlyn cocked her head to the side and laughed in response to his laugh.

"When Tim Townsend didn't start making crude jokes from the first day at the library, I should have known. I just assumed he hadn't seen her, but I should have known that Townsend wouldn't have missed a twenty-two-year-old college student with blazing-red hair."

"I'm not being jealous, Mark, but it sounds as though you really were attracted to her."

"No ... she doesn't have your stunning curves, she's too short, and too young —" He laughed again. "Actually, now that I know the truth, she's too old. She's almost the same age as my mother. Captain Davis evidently had dated her all through high school until she hooked up with your mom's beau." Mark stopped, realizing what he'd only briefly thought about the previous evening. "They all went to high school together. Which means they all knew each other. Which means that Davis and your mother knew each other."

"What are you talking about?"

Mark forgot he was talking with one of the suspects' family members, and sadly, Laura Allan was a suspect. Yes, Ashlyn was his fiancée, but if her mother was a murderer, he couldn't cover up her crime.

"We need to go inside," Mark said, attempting to keep the urgency he felt out of his tone. He didn't want to upset his pregnant fiancée any more than he probably already had.

CHAPTER 19

Mark scrutinized Laura Allan, hoping to get a baseline for her body language during normal conversation as she made small talk over their meal.

Body language — if you knew the person's usual mannerisms, gestures, and facial expressions — could be just as effective as a lie detector, if not more so. He could still read a stranger's body language, but some actions were hard to discern. If a person was insecure, an interviewer could misconstrue normal actions of crossing arms and legs or not looking a person in the eye, as lying, when the person might just be accustomed to shielding themselves from the world.

Laura was anything but shy and insecure. She was bold, and more often than not, she usually dominated the conversation, turning every discussion back to her. Tonight, however, everything seemed strained, as if she wanted to speak, but wasn't sure how to broach a subject. Not only did she nod and smile at everything Ashlyn and he said — without adding her own personal anecdotes — but she nervously darted her eyes around the room, as though she suspected someone may overhear her words and come crashing through the door.

"So, how was Gregory?" she finally asked midway through the meal without either Ashlyn or Mark prompting the question. Mark hadn't even known that Ashlyn told her mother that he'd gone to speak with Gregory Burke this morning.

"Fine, I suppose," Mark said. "Last time we spoke he'd looked older, but his son had just died. I'd imagine losing someone you loved would hurt. Especially after tragically losing his fiancée so many years ago."

Laura nodded. "Yes, and having an only child, like me. I can't imagine losing Ashlyn." She reached over and squeezed her daughter's hand, and Ashlyn looked as shocked at receiving the attention as Laura did for offering it. It was clear that they didn't hug when they saw each other. Unlike Mark and his mom, who if they hadn't seen each other for more than a few days, there was always a good, long hug before anything else.

Mark decided just to throw his first question out there and watch her response. "So, Laura, do you think Gregory killed his fiancée?"

Laura almost choked on her food. "Why on earth would you think that? Jessica's father killed her and her mother. Gregory was devastated."

Mark tilted his head just slightly to show his interest in her comment. The more interested a detective appeared in a suspect, not necessarily the situation, the more likely a person was to open up. "Oh, really, did you talk with Gregory after her death?"

Out of his peripherals, Mark saw Ashlyn's head turn back and forth, as though she were watching a tennis match.

"Well, no, he wouldn't take my calls. Not until a few years later, but that's because he was so devastated."

"Did you know Jessica?"

"Barely. She was a grade below us, so I was too busy being a cheerleader and all."

"I'll bet," Mark said, struggling to keep the sarcasm out of his voice, but knowing he'd failed.

Ashlyn tapped his knee under the table, and he

knew without looking at her that she was saying, "See what I've had to put up with?" He squeezed her hand to let her know he understood.

"So, Laura," he continued. "Since you were so busy in high school, did you ever talk to Jessica after you graduated?"

She took a sip of water before answering. "Not really. Maybe once or twice in the library."

He nodded, knowing she'd just told him a half-truth. "How 'bout Andrew Davis? Did you know him?"

This time her head jerked up from her plate. "Is there something you're trying to ask me, Mark?"

Mark shook his head, working to keep his expression innocent and open. He should have known that as shallow as the woman was, she was probably still intelligent and would see through his queries.

"Not really," he lied lightly, "but it's kind of nice that you know all these people I know. You can be of great help to me understanding their character. It just seems that if Andrew Davis was in the same grade as you, played football and all, that you would have known him too. So it interests me."

Laura pulled in a breath and swallowed, then went back for more water. "Yes. I knew Andrew. He was actually one of the first kids I met when I started at Edenbury high school."

"Did you two ever date?"

At that question, Laura laughed. "I'm sorry. Don't get me wrong, he was cute and all, but he wasn't my type."

"Meaning?" Mark prompted, surprised that Laura hadn't shut him down yet. He knew what type Davis wasn't, but he wanted to hear her say it. It made him wonder what lengths she would take to get the man she wanted.

"Well, you know ... I just didn't see a future with him. No offense, Mark, you're great, but back then, I didn't see myself with a cop."

Mark digested that piece of information. Davis obviously wasn't a cop in high school, so Laura had slipped forward a few years, it seemed. "So, how many times did you go out?"

Ashlyn looked at him, and he squeezed her leg gently to let her know he knew what he was doing. But then again, she probably wouldn't be too happy if she knew what he was doing.

Laura made a few noises but didn't actually say anything. She knew he'd caught her in her blunder, but evidently, she wasn't a very good liar and was afraid to talk.

"It's okay, Laura. I know you went out a few times," he said. On the surface, it was a lie, but since he was ninety-nine percent sure they'd dated, it didn't feel like a lie.

Not that it mattered. A common misbelief among criminals was that police officers had to tell the truth. When in fact, they could say just about anything they wanted to get a confession, as long as they didn't threaten the suspect or fabricate evidence. Often he'd found if he acted as though he understood the suspect's crime, identified with their plight, they'd open up to him and confess.

Laura dropped her head. "We didn't really go out. We just happened across each other one night. He was upset; I was upset ..." she trailed off.

As much as Mark wanted to prompt her to continue, he held off, hoping she'd feel compelled to finish her statement.

"It was a long time ago." Laura rested her fork on the plate, slid her chair back, and left the dining room. After a few seconds, he heard her bedroom door shut.

"What the heck is going on?" Ashlyn's eyes were round as the conversation started to make sense.

"Wait!" She grabbed his hand. "Mark, you don't think —"

Mark just shook his head and expelled a breath he felt as though he'd been holding the entire meal so he could hear every word Laura said.

"Mom and Captain Davis dated? And their exes were engaged to each other? Mark, you're wrong. There's no way that my mother —" Ashlyn pushed back her chair.

"Ashlyn ..." He touched her hand.

Tears poured down her cheeks. "I can't believe you just interrogated my mother over dinner."

"It wasn't like that —"

"It was *exactly* like that," she seethed, pulling her hand out from underneath his and turning to leave.

Mark jumped out of his chair and blocked her path. "Okay, it was something like that, but not because I believe your mother is guilty."

He checked himself for a second, making sure he was telling the truth. Yes, he believed Laura was innocent. He didn't feel she had a motive to kill Jessica. And if she did possess information that the Burkes were responsible for her grandmother's murder, he truly believed she would have announced it to the world years ago. Not that that was a great quality, but in his eyes, it did decrease her motive.

He squeezed Ashlyn's hands, hoping she'd hear him out. "Please forgive me. I should have asked you. But what I think is that your mother may have information. And I'm sorry. That may have been the wrong way of going about getting answers, but it really is the most effective way."

Ashlyn sighed loudly. "Okay, Mark. I forgive you, but rule number one if I'm going to marry you is that there will be no interviewing of me or my family members on our personal time." She crossed her arms and rested them on her belly.

"Rule number one?" he probed. "How many rules will there be?"

"You're doing it again. Just like you did the other day. Stop reading between the lines."

Mark scratched his head. "But that wasn't reading between the lines. Stating a number and a rule denotes that there are more rules to follow."

"Ugh!" Ashlyn threw up her hands and started to walk around him. "You're incorrigible!"

Mark reached out for her and pulled her back to him carefully. Luckily she didn't walk too quickly in her current condition. "Okay. Rule number one. I promise not to interrogate you, your mother, or your aunt in our home, but my skills can be very effective when it comes to boys." He touched her beautiful round belly. "Trust me, you'll want my skills by the time he reaches five." Ashlyn dropped her head on his chest, and he wrapped his arms around her. "I'm sorry, Ash. I won't do it again. Do you want me to go apologize?"

"No. She probably doesn't even realize what you were doing. She's just upset over Gregory Burke." She looked up at him. "She really loved him. I don't have the heart to tell her they're first cousins. That'll really screw her up. Luckily, it doesn't sound as if they did anything. I guess she'd had a plan for a prom-night after-party, though."

"Eww ..." Mark couldn't help himself. "I don't have any cousins, but that just seems too weird."

"It's not like they knew."

"Let's hope not."

Ashlyn pulled back. "I have to go talk to her."

"Yeah." Mark felt like kicking himself. He could have held off his interrogation until breakfast, and then maybe Ashlyn and he could have had another fun night fooling around like a couple of teenagers.

Impulsive.

CHAPTER 20

Ashlyn leaned against Mark most of the trip home, but she didn't speak but a few sentences here and there. He'd been an idiot to think he could interrogate her mother in front of her without her knowing it.

As Mark entered Edenbury's city limits, he brushed the hair away from Ashlyn's face. She'd fallen asleep with her head against his shoulder, and her hair had fallen over her face like a veil hiding her from the outside world. "You awake?"

She peered up at him with a sleepy-eyed grin. "No. I had the best dream."

"Really?" That was good. If she was having a good dream, she couldn't be too upset with him. "What was it about?"

Ashlyn sat up and adjusted her clothes, making sure her belly was covered. It amazed him how aware of her belly she was, even though she was pregnant.

She let out a long sigh and then rested her head against the headrest. "We were somewhere in the Caribbean. The water was the bluest green I've ever seen, and we could see fish swimming on the bottom. I was wearing a skimpy string bikini, I had a flat stomach, and my navel was in how it should be."

Mark couldn't help the laugh that burst out of his throat, even though he knew it'd probably enrage her.

She smacked his shoulder. "It's not funny."

"Actually, it is. I dream of gun battles and ghosts, and you're upset because you're dreaming about yourself in a bikini, wondering if you'll ever wear one again."

"That's a nightmare for a woman, Mark."

Mark shook his head. "Ashlyn, you're going to look awesome — you look great now," he amended quickly. "You're young. Your body is going to bounce right back into shape." He touched her belly. "And even if it doesn't, you'll still look great. And I happen to think one-piece suits are sexier anyway. I even like that little skirt you wore over your swimsuit this summer."

He wiggled his eyebrows. "It's mysterious, makes me wonder what's beneath the skirt."

"Men!" she said, as if exasperated with all men, not just him. "You guys are so ridiculous. You've seen women naked a thousand times, and still, every man acts as though there's something enigmatic between a woman's legs."

"Well, women's brains are definitely enigmatic."

Ashlyn lowered the visor and inspected her face in the mirror. "So, what do we do next?"

"We?"

"You said we were going to get a marriage license today ..." she paused, looking over at his side of the truck, "but if you changed your mind ..."

He huffed out a breath. "No, I didn't change my mind, and I know I called in sick, but I do have to do a couple of things at the office when we get back."

His lovely wife-to-be dropped her head and looked up at him beneath her lowered brow with a scowl that'd get most criminals to confess. "You're kidding, right?" She crossed her arms. "I thought we were going to have a special day."

"We are ..." He reached for her hand. "I just have a few things to check on with Townsend. Matter of fact, I'll stop by the courthouse and get the papers so we can fill them out at home and then we'll take them in together." Mark stopped at a red light and turned to see her lip jutted out in a pout. "I did say we'd sneak away this weekend."

"I know. I just thought we'd have a special night."

"We will. I'll drop you off so you can get all dolled up, then I'll pick you up this afternoon and we'll do something special."

She released a long sigh. "Okay. I could use a nap anyway."

Mark laughed. She'd slept almost the entire trip. "Perfect. Your place or mine?"

"Mine, in case I need my car."

Mark took the next left and weaved through Ashlyn's townhome complex. He parked in front of her single-car garage and turned to her. "So … your place or mine this weekend?"

"I thought we were going away."

He reached over and unbuckled the seatbelt, then gently coaxed her to his side of the truck. Brushing her hair off her shoulder, exposing her slender neck, he touched his lips just below her ear. "We'll be married this weekend. So I was sort of hoping you might actually want to live with me."

"Oh … yes … umm … wow. I wasn't thinking."

The Library

Mark moved so that his face was directly in front of hers. He closed his mouth gently on her top lip then her bottom, tugging lightly the way she liked. She opened up to him after a couple of seconds and their tongues moved together in an almost primal dance, as if they could make love merely with a kiss. Mark broke the connection first and worked his way back to her ear. "I'm looking forward to you falling asleep in my arms every night and waking up beside me for as long as we both shall live."

"Oh, Mark ..." Ashlyn said through a breathy sigh of satisfaction. She lifted her head, giving him better access to her neck. "Wherever you want. God, how did I find you?"

His lips turned up against her skin in a contented grin. It wasn't a rehearsed line; he'd meant every word. But he loved that he could cause that reaction in her.

As much as Mark didn't want to leave Ashlyn's side, he knew that he had to. This weekend they'd marry and be together every night. But right now, he needed to check something in his father's files. Something that the captain had said had been nagging at him.

Not only did he think he knew who killed Wade Buchanan, he was almost certain he knew why Jessica and her mother had been murdered too.

CHAPTER 21

Mark called Townsend as he made his way toward the police station. Since it was a few minutes before four, the older detective would still be there. The one thing that man did dutifully was follow his schedule.

Unless they were in the middle of a crime scene, Townsend was like clockwork. He'd clock in at exactly eight a.m., leave for lunch at 11:59, be sitting back behind his desk at 12:59, then at four o'clock on the dot, he'd clock out to go home. If Townsend was out knocking on doors, however, Mark couldn't trust where he'd end up.

"Detective Townsend," his partner answered his office line. If Mark wasn't mistaken, he sounded downright cheerful. Must have had a good lunch.

Maybe he met a nice waitress at his favorite diner. He'd dated almost every one of the women who worked there. The woman never seemed to be upset with him, though, so they must have done the breaking up.

"Well, you sound chipper," Mark said. "You must have had a good weekend."

Townsend laughed, a deep belly laugh, the type that always made Mark smile. "Wife took me back again, and I swear we had the best time. I don't know how she can be so sweet and funny one minute and then have her claws out the next."

Mark knew why Townsend's wife bared her claws. Because she gave him everything, but he'd only be content for a few days. So when Townsend started behaving like a tomcat, she probably started treating him as if he were nothing but an animal. Mark held his tongue, though.

"Wonderful!" Mark said. "So, should I smack you upside the head next time you make googly eyes at some chica?"

"Yes!"

"Wow. You're serious about this. I'm impressed. So, did you get the message I left earlier?"

"Yep."

"And …?" Mark said. Townsend loved to play games with him whenever he was feeling superior.

"Just waitin' on you, man. You back in town yet?"

"On my way."

Once back at the station, Mark searched through the employee records and found what he was looking for. "Bingo!"

"You were right?" Townsend asked, peering over his shoulder. "You think they know each other?"

"Yep! Let's go."

Mark drove by an abandoned warehouse, then turned down the street that ran behind the library. The shelter served until five o'clock, according to Townsend. So more than likely, they allowed the homeless at least a half an hour to eat. Provided Townsend's info was correct, they were right on time.

The old man hadn't been living here. Too many rules. Probably the other reason he came right before they closed, hoping no one would try to reform him when he just wanted to fill his belly.

The four-story redbrick church was large enough to house many of the homeless, and according to his information, they had several other buildings in the area. The Catholic Church had worked diligently in providing housing and shelter, but sadly, there were still so many homeless people in the area.

Like Wade Buchanan, Mark imagined that many of the vagrants were homeless for reasons other than drug addiction and lack of employment. Clearly, a percentage of the homeless community was hiding from the law or other citizens. Whether it was for back child support payments owed, a felony warrant, or an abusive spouse or parent, some folks couldn't take the chance of someone recognizing them.

Mark parallel parked his unmarked cruiser in front of another car, leaving enough room at the rear of the space that he could get out quickly if someone parked in front of his vehicle.

Townsend hopped out of the passenger side. "I'll go around back and meet you on the other side of the building in case he sees you coming."

Mark nodded and made his slow way to the front of the building, giving Townsend enough time to get around the structure. At no less than 120-foot wide and 80-foot deep based on the amount of windows, it'd take Townsend a few minutes to make it around the building.

As Mark held back behind a paper birch, several

groups of men and women exited the church. He glanced at each one, not seeing the person he wanted.

Townsend strolled around the opposite end of the building, looking every bit like a cop. Not as much as Mark, but Townsend had never made the cut for UC either. And though he didn't look like it with his increased waistline, the man could run down a suspect if he had to. Not all of them, but he had a sixth sense when it came to knowing which direction the runner would take. He was also a crack shot. As many issues as Townsend had, if Mark had his choice, he'd choose him as his backup every time.

Townsend returned a head nod to several of the larger men who passed him. Ex-cons, no doubt. A slight head nod from a civilian meant, *I recognize you're a cop, and I'm cool.* When suspicious persons didn't make eye contact, however, Mark knew to question them.

The last person to exit was their man. Mark motioned to his partner, and Townsend swiftly closed the distance.

One look at Townsend, and Wild Bill changed directions, walking almost directly into Mark.

"Hey, Bill. Where ya goin'?" Mark asked with a smile.

The Library

Bill waved a hand at Mark as though he were waving away a fly and darted off down the side of the building.

Townsend saw and picked up speed, but Mark had already bolted after the man. "Just wanna talk to you, Bill. Don't make this difficult on yourself."

The old man ran a few more yards. But as Mark caught up with him, he whipped around, causing Mark to drop to a squat, drawing his gun. Mark exhaled and stood when he recognized that Bill had just been frustrated.

"Stupid old man!" Mark shouted. "You know better than to swing around on a cop like that. I might have shot you."

Bill shrugged. "What the hell do you want? I told you everything the other day."

Townsend jogged up to Mark, doing his best to control his breathing.

"No, you didn't. Let's go."

Bill planted his feet firmly in a fighter's stance, but then crossed his arms. "I ain't going anywhere unless you have a warrant for my arrest."

"I can still arrest you for trespassing, Bill. I have the paperwork; I just didn't process it."

The man shrugged again. "Go ahead."

Mark knew Wild Bill was beyond intimidating, but he figured it was worth a try. "Buy you a cup of coffee, then?"

"I don't have time. I got someplace I need to be."

"Need a lift? We'll talk in the car."

The old man huffed out a laugh. "What d'ya want from me, Detective?"

Mark lifted his chin. "A friend of mine said you did him a favor."

Bill waved his hand again and turned to walk off.

Mark trotted after him. "Wesley Burke Jr., you know him?"

Wild Bill stopped again, crossing his arms a second time, probably to resist throwing a punch. "You're not dealing with a moron, Detective. Yes, I know the Burkes. Is there a soul in this part of the state who doesn't? But no, he didn't tell you I did him any favors."

Mark watched carefully as Bill rattled off his words. He was lying, of course. But what could Mark do other than watch his reaction?

Bill turned to leave again, so Mark made one more attempt. "You were never paid, were you? Because you never found what he wanted, huh?"

The old man turned around again. "Not that I give

a rat's ass about what you're trying to pin on me, but where are you getting your information?"

Mark laughed. "You sound like Captain Davis."

Bill narrowed his eyes ever so slightly, and Mark's heart skipped a beat. He'd hit a nerve.

CHAPTER 22

Mark removed two keys from his ring then handed the set to Townsend. "Take the car back to the station, grab the two files in my top drawer and show them to Captain Davis, then you and he need to meet me back at the library."

Townsend raised his hands as though he were confused. "You expect the captain to come without any explanation?"

"Yes. Just tell him I'll be at the library, and he'll come."

"And you expect me to leave you alone?"

Mark sighed. "Yes. There's something I have to do on my own."

"Don't do anything stupid, Waters. The homeless

community doesn't have anything to lose, so be careful. Don't try to take down that guy on your own."

A tad insulted, Mark raised an eyebrow at the man who'd done stupid things most of his life. When had Mark ever done anything stupid? Besides hooking up with the dispatcher, that is. Other than that, he'd never done anything irresponsible. In fact, he was too serious most of the time. Before he'd helped solve his father's murder and met Ashlyn, life had been downright boring. He'd thrown his life into work, helped run his mother's business, slept, and ate.

Townsend raised his hands in an apologetic gesture — or maybe it was a self-defense response, thinking Mark might hit him. "Hear me out, Mark. You've been acting rather strange lately. I know Ashlyn's probably moody and all, but trust me ... it's just the hormones. She'll be right as rain in about six months."

"I'm not acting strange," Mark shot back, but then honed in on Townsend's words. "Six months? She'll have the baby in a month."

Townsend stepped forward and patted Mark's upper arm with a fatherly tap. "No one mentioned postpartum depression?"

Mark moved out from underneath his partner's hand and jogged off. He really didn't want to take advice from a man whose marriage had failed repeatedly. "I don't have time for this. Ashlyn and I are fine. I have a murder to solve, and besides, Wild Bill's not homeless."

"What?" Townsend called behind him, but Mark didn't have time to stop and chat. "Work isn't your life, Waters. Remember that."

Mark waved him off and bolted down the street toward the library. He could have had Townsend drop him off. But by the time he'd backtracked to the cruiser, he could have been there. Besides, it allowed him time to think about the situation. Once he found the one missing piece, he was positive the rest of the pieces would fall into place — or come out of the woodwork looking for it perhaps.

Using his key, Mark let himself inside the library. He was relieved that Jay wasn't there to meet him outside as she'd done before. He hoped that proved he'd conjured up her image somehow. Maybe he'd seen her face on TV when he was a child and it had been in his subconscious all these years.

"Hi, Mark."

He nearly jumped out of his skin. He looked up. "Damn! I'd really hoped I wouldn't have to commit myself after I solved your murder."

The Library

She smiled from her position on the balcony. Fiction, as she'd told him several times. He walked up the stairs slowly again, his heart nearly throbbing through his chest. She'd not done anything to scare him, and she didn't look like a half-decayed corpse, so why did he feel so nervous?

"You don't need to be committed, Mark. I don't know why, but you can see me. Just like you saw Edda."

"Edda. No, I never saw Edda."

"She said you knew she was there. You heard her when she tried to talk to you, and you felt her when she tried to connect, and then you saw her image when no one else could."

"How do you know about that? Do you ghosts get together?"

She smiled. "No. We can only be where we once were. She's been here, so she can materialize here if someone summons her by thinking about her. I saw her when I was investigating her murder, but she came in the form of a child, since that was one of the ages she was when she was here alive, I guess. I didn't know she was the child I'd seen until I saw her in my current state. She explained to me that she'd watched me, hoped that I could solve her murder and set her free. I don't think we're really here, though. I think just a part of our psyche is here to help solve our murders. I've never seen another soul. Just Edda. But she told me if I ever saw you that you could help me."

Mark closed his eyes and shook his head. "I just can't believe this is happening. Why me?"

Jay shook her head. "I don't know either. I've tried to attack the person who killed me, but all I can do is torment them by moving light objects." She smiled again. "That was me the other day, with the microfilm. Someone was here looking again. They'd trashed the place the night before, but then came back the next day and started going through the files. It's not there. I moved it before I died. But the cases were light enough and I was mad enough, that I was able to throw them at the murderer."

"Enough with the games, then, Jay. If you saw the murderer, just tell me."

"I don't know. The person who comes here is always wearing a mask. But whoever it is knows my name, and said 'sorry' the last time."

"Was it male or female?"

"It's weird. As I said, I don't think I'm really here. I think I'm in another dimension. I can see you and hear you, but your voice comes through as a garbled echo, as if it's going through a chamber of some sort.

And slow. I know you think you're talking at regular speed, but in my dimension, your words come through individually, as if a tape recorder is on slow speed."

Mark laughed. "Tape recorder. You really are from the eighties." A bit settled at their almost normal conversation, he worked his way closer to her. "I believe you hid some information here."

She nodded. "But I don't remember where it is. This was my favorite spot, though, so it has to be here."

"Yes, that's what I figured too." Mark made his way down the aisle where Jay had sat the other day. If she'd hidden it here, how was it possible that no one had ever found it? He touched the different bindings, looking for anything that she might have chosen. The film was thin, so she could have placed it in the back of any book. Certainly, she'd hidden the microfilm inside the thick cover of an old fairy tale. "Tell me," he said as he pored over the titles, "why didn't you tell your father?"

"He couldn't hear me."

"But I thought you played chess."

"We did. I'd motion which piece I wanted to move, and he could feel my urging I guess, but he could never hear me speak. But he would talk to me. Somehow, he knew I was here. I think that's why he came back."

"Came back?"

"Yes. He'd hidden out here the first few nights, but then he ran. He came back six months ago. He wanted to tell me that Gregory's son had died."

Mark looked up from the books he was inspecting. "Why do you think he would do that?"

"He'd said it didn't make sense. He liked Gregory. He didn't think he'd ever hurt me, but for the life of him — his exact words — he couldn't figure out why anyone would kill us. Unlike the rest of the town, who'd immediately pinned our murders on my father, he knew the truth, and so did I. My father had come home that night and found my mother tied up. It had to have been a man. He'd knocked on the door, and like an idiot, I answered without looking. He had a mask on, so I couldn't see his face. But he was tall. He grabbed me as soon as I opened the door, tied my hands behind my back, and then did the same to my mother."

Mark stood up. "The idea that someone could kill anyone, let alone two innocent women —" He shook his head. "I think I know who did it. I just need the evidence."

"The man was scared, Mark. When my father came home, he was startled. I don't think he planned to murder us. He just wanted to know where I'd hidden the information. But my father came home ... he'd had us both in my mother's room ... and when my father saw us strapped to the bed, he ran toward the bed, and the man hit him with a long rod of some sort. My mother wouldn't stop screaming. She thought the man had killed my father, and the next thing I knew he had a gun aimed at her head, shouting at her to stop screaming. But she wouldn't." Jay dropped her head, as if she were crying. "She wouldn't stop screaming, so he shot her. I didn't even breathe when he turned the gun on me. I just shook my head and said, 'please,' and he pulled the trigger." She shook her head again. "I didn't want to die. I was so happy. I was living the dream, engaged to the prince. I was going to win the Game of Life, as my father had always called it. My father told me how hard he'd struggled, but he didn't want me to want for anything."

Mark stepped toward her. "I'm sorry, Jay. I only know one way to help you now. I want to make them pay. Where did you put the information? I think I know why they want it. How can you remember all those details and not this one thing?"

She glided past him like a cool breeze. She said she couldn't be any place where she hadn't been alive, so why had he felt her in his apartment? The idea was disturbing, as he realized he was attracted to her because she reminded him of Ashlyn. He knew immediately something was odd about her, the reason her breath had felt cool, even in his dreams.

Jay climbed the steps to the top of the ladder.

Of course, he realized. She would have chosen something out of the way. He climbed up behind her. The moment he reached her step, her body dematerialized into mist as he moved through her. All he felt was a cool breeze as if her presence had brushed his skin.

"Which one?" Mark read off the titles, looking for anything that was popular when Jay was a college student.

A vision flashed in his head. It was Jay, climbing up the ladder. He saw her shove a book back onto the shelf as she looked around her, but once again, he couldn't see the title.

Mark ran his fingers along the spines of the books, grazing over the titles. There were just too many of them. What would a twenty-two-year-old girl have read in the eighties? "Wait!" he said to no one in particular, since Jay had disappeared again.

The Library

He pulled out his phone and dialed the person who would know.

His mother answered on the first ring. "Hi, sweetheart."

"Hi, Mom. Not to be abrupt, but I need something from you."

"Okay."

"What books were you reading in the eighties?"

She laughed.

"Mom ..." he tried not to whine, but for some reason, his mother was the one woman he could whine to until he got his way. "This is serious. I'm in a situation, and I need to know what was popular around the mid-eighties." He looked at the books on the shelf. "An author's name that starts with S maybe?"

"Hmm ... okay. Let me think. Well, my favorite will always be Sidney Sheldon. I think he was the first to blend romance with suspense. And he always had a great female heroine."

Mark thrilled to see all of Sheldon's books were right in front of his eyes. He read off the titles until one jumped out at him: *Master of the Game*.

CHAPTER 23

"*Master of the Game*," he repeated aloud. *The Game of Life*, Jay had said. He was sure he had the correct book.

"That was a great one," his mother said over the phone. "Epic. The story swept through several generations. About greed, betrayal, family. Loved it!"

Chills swept down Mark's arms. "Thanks, Mom. I think this is it. I'll call you later." He hung up without explanation, knowing she'd understand, and made his way back down the ladder. Once at the bottom, he sat in the same chair where Jay had sat the other day.

Ignoring the urge to jump to the back of the book, knowing he had the correct one, Mark traced the white letters on the faded-blue spine. The cover was a plain off-white. No image. The dust jacket had been thrown away years ago, he assumed. He opened the book and looked at the date on the copyright page. 1982. Perfect! It was an enormous book. As his mother had said, epic. Probably close to five hundred pages.

Unable to wait a second longer, Mark flipped to the back of the book. Tracing the endpaper pasted to the back cover, running his index finger over the slight edge beneath the cream-colored paper, he thrilled at the fact that he was correct. Something was beneath the paperboard.

Mark tore at the glued border at the top, carefully lifting the edges along the header. His fingers were too big to pull it open just a little, and he fretted over the fact that he was destroying a book. He loved books. Well, at least it wasn't a first-edition book that he couldn't replace.

He turned the book upside down, attempting to get the thin sheets of film to slide out.

"Did you find —"

"Gah!" he screamed, dropping the book. "Stop sneaking up on me."

Jay stepped closer. "I loved that novel. I should have remembered."

Willing his heart to slow, Mark went back to work on the book. "I don't suppose you could will these out, so I don't destroy this book any more than I already have."

As if she didn't find what he'd said funny, she just shook her head.

Giving up, Mark pulled the thick paper backing down completely, freeing several transparent brown pieces of microfilm and a white sheet of notepad paper with handwritten notes.

"Ahh …" he said. "The missing piece. *Why.*" He sighed, not wanting to believe his speculation; though he knew he had enough evidence now to put the pieces together.

"I'll take that." He heard the voice, hating that he recognized it.

Mark looked up to see a gun pointed at his head, her hand held out.

"You know I didn't hurt her, right?" Mrs. Davis said.

Mark nodded and then shook his head. "Why didn't you say anything?"

"Who would have believed me, Markey? Not without the evidence. If I'd mentioned that I thought Jessica had taken evidence that would have saved my library, then I would have looked guilty. I needed you and your team to find them before anyone else did. If he didn't think I had proof that would convict him, he would have killed me too."

Mark shook his head.

"Markey, I might not be able to shoot you, but my friend can."

"You can come out now, Bill. I know you're beside her. You put on a good show, but I knew you weren't homeless," Mark said.

Bill stepped around the aisle of books and smiled. "You're a nice kid, Mark. Don't make me hurt you."

"Blackmail?" Mark smiled. "All comes down to money, huh?"

Bill stepped forward and grabbed the film and scrap of paper from Mark.

And then Mark heard a hammer of a gun locking into place. The second wave of the party had arrived. He hoped the third wave wouldn't take too long.

"Drop the gun, Margaret. Let's go. All of you," the older man said. He snatched the papers out of Bill's hand and motioned the three of them out of the aisle.

Margaret dropped the gun and backed away with Bill shielding her.

"Dammit!" the man shouted. "You just couldn't leave well enough alone, could you? All of you!"

"She came to you, didn't she?" Mark asked the man.

He didn't know why, but a heavy weight filled his chest. As mad as he was, even though he'd never known Jay personally, he felt tears threaten. He never cried. But knowing that this man had betrayed so many people. That so many people had suffered and died because of him caused his insides to battle within him. And the hurt wasn't over. The man had left a legacy that he would now be a part of forever. Someday, Mark would have to explain to his son — Ashlyn's son — the family's horrible secret.

Mark stepped toward the man. "It can stop now. Devin has an unborn son. You can make a difference in his life."

The man's eyes watered up for a brief second. "Ashlyn? The girl at the bar?"

Mark nodded.

"Devin told me he broke up with her. I don't believe you. More lies." The man raised the gun, but then stopped. "Where did you come from?" he asked, waving the gun at the little girl to move out of the way.

Mark smiled as he saw the young girl in a long dress. She had long braided hair tied back with a bright blue ribbon that matched her vintage dress. She turned and smiled at Mark, then turned back to Burke.

Obviously confused, Burke narrowed his eyes at the

little girl, then jerked his head up as Jay walked toward him. "No. It can't be. You're dead." He aimed the gun and shot, but Jay continued toward him.

Mark motioned Mrs. Davis and Bill back toward the stairs as Burke concentrated on the two women closing in on him.

"I ... killed ... you. You ... you ... can't be here," Burke stuttered. "And who the hell are you?" he shouted at the little girl again.

"Oh, that's right, you never met Edda. Did you?" Jay said. "Because she was murdered ... just like you murdered me. But you knew all about her, didn't you? Wasn't she beautiful? Just like her granddaughter, Laura, and great granddaughter, Ashlyn. Heirs to your fortune. I tried to protect you from Mrs. Davis smearing your good name and that cop you hired who turned on you. I overheard them and came to you, and you betrayed me." Jay moved closer and Burke instinctively stepped back. "You killed my mother, you killed me, and then you came back and killed my father."

Burke shot again and again, but Jay and Edda continued to back him up against the railing. Then he stopped and turned the gun toward Mark. "I'll kill them," he warned.

A shot rang out and Mark dropped, along with Bill who pulled Margaret down beside him.

Not hearing anything, Mark patted down his body, looking for gunshot wounds. He'd heard stories how many officers didn't even know they'd been shot until they were bleeding out. He released a breath of relief when his hands were dry. He checked Bill and Margaret, who were prone beside him. Bill nodded, the ex-cop in him comprehending what Mark needed to know without words.

Gun drawn now, Mark glanced around the half-wall connected to the steps. Burke was on the ground. The ghosts were gone. Had Burke shot himself instead? Or had Jay killed him somehow? Her revenge had been powerful enough that Burke had been able to see her. But had she actually been able to pull the trigger?

"You okay, Mark?" Townsend shouted from below.

Townsend, Mark sighed inwardly. The third wave had made it right in time. "Yeah ..." Mark slowly stood and inched his way toward Burke's lifeless body. He kicked the gun out of the way and knelt over Mr. Burke, checking his pulse. "I'm fine. Burke's dead, though." Mark inspected the wound. Townsend had made a clean CNS shot. Townsend had always been one of the best at the target range.

Mark dropped his head, realizing he was going to have to deliver the news to Ashlyn. First, that Burke was dead. And second, that she was, in fact, heir to one of the wealthiest families in Pennsylvania. He didn't know how he felt about that. He hoped that she wouldn't want any of it.

Mark pulled himself upright again and walked back over to a crying Mrs. Davis and Bill comforting her. "Do you want to wait until your husband gets here?"

Margaret whipped her gaze up to him. "What do you mean?"

"You're both under arrest for conspiracy, blackmail, and obstruction of justice."

She bolted to her feet. "What?"

"Give it a rest, Margaret," Captain Davis ordered as he climbed the steps.

"How long have you been here?" Mrs. Davis asked in a whisper.

"Long enough." Davis turned her around and proceeded to handcuff his wife, while Mark handcuffed Wild Bill. Davis assisted his wife down the stairs as tears — real tears this time — streamed down her pale cheeks. Davis stepped in front of her at the bottom of the steps. "By the way, I'll be filing for divorce first thing in the morning." He looked up at Wild Bill, who was a tall man, taller than all of them. He sneered his distaste for the both of them. "For the library? For him? Of all the people you could have hooked up with. What a piece of work you are, Margaret."

"We're just friends, Andrew," Mrs. Davis said.

Captain Davis pushed Wild Bill forward and the man obeyed; though, he turned around and glared at him. "We've been friends longer than you've been married, Davis."

Davis said nothing as he followed the two of them toward the exit.

Townsend passed them and worked his way up the stairs toward Mark. "I called the meat wagon."

Mark just nodded as he looked down at the old man. "Sad. He wouldn't have gone to jail if he'd come clean twenty-five years ago. Yeah, the Burke name would have been smeared, and he'd lose half his assets, but murder? For money? She was so beautiful."

"Yeah." Townsend agreed, then nudged Mark in the arm. "Hey, who was he talking to?"

Mark exhaled a deep breath. "Jessica Buchanan."

"The dead girl?"

The Library

Mark glanced around the library. Jay was gone and so was Edda. He'd solved both of their murders, so they didn't need to hang around anymore, he guessed. "The dead girl has a name, Townsend. He was talking to Jay."

"You say that as if you actually saw her too."

Mark looked at the older detective and smiled. His comment didn't require an answer. "Nice shot, by the way. Glad you didn't forget about me here."

Townsend smacked him on the back. "When have I ever not backed you up?"

"True." And it was. Townsend may have made a lot of mistakes, but he was a good cop when push came to shove — literally.

"You wanna get a drink after we finish up here?" Townsend asked.

Mark sighed. And yet, some things never changed. "Go home to your wife, Tim. Ashlyn's waiting on me."

"Yeah, I guess you're right," he muttered.

EPILOGUE

A knock on the doorjamb caused Mark to look up.

Gregory Burke and his wife, Jacqueline, stood in the open doorway, blue and yellow balloons in one hand, a teddy bear too large for a day-old newborn in the other. "Can we come in?"

"Hey ... Of course, come in," Ashlyn whispered, careful not to jostle the tiny bundle in her arms.

Jacqueline tiptoed toward the bed, her eyes immediately filling. "Oh," she fanned her eyes, "I can't tell you how happy ..." She blinked back the tears. "Can I hold him?"

Ashlyn nodded, allowing her son's grandmother to hold her pride and joy.

"He's so beautiful. He looks just like you, Ashlyn."

The Library

Mark smiled. He did. There wasn't a trace of Burke in his son. If it weren't for the fact that he was heir to the Burke fortune via Ashlyn, they'd probably demand a blood test. But the Burkes were so happy to have a grandson they probably wouldn't have even requested it then.

Gregory Burke wrapped his arm around his wife and pulled the blanket away from the baby boy's face. "Hi, Jayden." Burke looked up at Ashlyn. "Is that right? Jayden."

Ashlyn smiled. "Yes. It means *thankful*."

"I like it," Burke said, making eye contact with Mark.

Mark knew what he was thinking. Jayden ... like Jay. And yes, Jayden's friends might shorten his name when he grows up. But no, Mark hadn't suggested the name; Ashlyn did. But he liked it. He felt Jay had saved his life by allowing herself to be seen by Gregory's father, Wesley Burke Jr. Edda's being there hadn't hurt either. She definitely stopped the first bullet, but it was Jay's presence that had unnerved Mr. Burke. Looking into the eyes of the woman you'd shot in cold blood would drive anyone mad.

Mark had a good idea that if Townsend hadn't shot Burke, Jay and Edda would have somehow made sure he'd gone over the balcony before he'd pulled the trigger on Mark, though. At least that's why he thought they'd been edging toward the railing.

Mark walked around the hospital bed and stood next to his wife. "Yeah. I like it too. We have a lot to be thankful for."

"Hey," another voice said, walking around the doorway. Captain Davis held a bright blue gift bag and balloons with *Congratulations* printed on the outside. He lowered the bag over a side table at the end of the room, but looked at the woman who followed in behind him before setting it down. "Is this all right?" he asked Mark's mom.

"Perfect. Where's my grandbaby?" Cheryl Lynn asked as she scooted up next to the Burkes. "Oh, he's so adorable. Can I hold him?"

Everyone looked to Ashlyn, as if the seven-pound bundle of blankets was explosive.

"Of course you can, Mom," Ashlyn said.

If it were possible, his mother glowed. She always had a beautiful blush and was always chipper, but today she was in her glory. Whether it was from Ashlyn calling her "mom," as she'd suggested the moment Mark and Ashlyn had told her they'd officially tied the knot, or holding a newborn baby in her arms, he couldn't tell. But then Mark also saw how close Captain Davis was standing to his mother.

The two men made eye contact, and Mark made sure he gave his superior his best, *You better not hurt my mother* look. It'd only been a month since Davis had filed for divorce, but he'd moved out of his house the day after he'd arrested his wife. He'd admitted that he'd known since the beginning that Margaret had been hiding something in the case, probably the reason she'd become so chummy with him. But he'd been lonely, he admitted. And Margaret had been an attractive woman.

Mark sat down on the bed next to his wife and kissed her on the forehead. "I love you."

"I love you too," she said, smiling up at him. "Looks like we might have another seat filled on Thanksgiving," she whispered.

He laughed. "Looks that way."

As soon as Mark finished speaking with the district attorney after Margaret Davis' arrest, he headed to see the woman he'd always admired. The DA had mixed feelings about pressing charges against Margaret Davis or William "Wild Bill" James. If tried and convicted, they could end up serving ten years, but he doubted he had enough to convict either of them and didn't think the public would appreciate the tax dollars it'd take to go to trial.

Yes, they'd tried to blackmail Wesley Burke Jr., but they hadn't known when Bill had told Burke that Jay had the information, not Margaret, that Burke would go after Jay.

According to Mrs. Davis, Wesley Burke Jr. had originally hired Bill to find out who was blackmailing him. He'd found Bill from his good friend, who happened to be the commissioner. The commissioner had told Burke about Bill, who'd recently left the police department and gone into private investigation. After all, the commissioner had been out of the department a long time, so he hadn't known about Bill's illegal activities on the job. The chief at the time had swept everything under the rug, according to Captain Davis.

When Jay had gone to Burke, attempting to protect his reputation, he'd assumed that she'd been the one who'd written the blackmail letter, Mrs. Davis surmised.

The one thing Mark had not figured out in all of this was how Mrs. Davis had figured out that Wesley Burke Senior had murdered Edda.

Surprisingly, when Mark had gone to the county

jail the day after her arrest, Mrs. Davis had been more than willing to talk with him. "Have a seat, Markey. I hold no ill will against you. I know you were just doing your job, and I really needed to find that evidence before he did, or my life would have been in danger too. Just like he killed Buck."

Mark wasn't so sure he believed the woman, but he pulled out a chair and took a seat across from Mrs. Davis. "Without the bullet or casing, there's no way to know for sure who killed Wade Buchanan. Since Burke admitted to shooting Jessica and her mother, and was ready to shoot us, we assume he did in fact kill Wade Buchanan. But I guess we'll never know. I assume someone who'd seen Wade Buchanan at the library must have tipped Burke off, and Burke, not wanting to leave any loose ends after all these years, must have shot him."

All the pieces had fit together nicely, but Mark wasn't convinced.

He leaned across the table, hoping to catch her confidence. Maybe he'd find a few more pieces to finish his puzzle. "From what I understand, Wade Buchanan heard that Devin Burke had died, so he came back into town, as he thought it was odd. I think he missed being near where he felt the strongest presence of his daughter."

Obviously not buying his guess on why Buchanan had come back to town, Mrs. Davis narrowed her eyes. "You saw her, didn't you?"

Mark glared back, wondering if it mattered. "Yes."

"I looked everywhere for those damn films. I'd always assumed she'd hidden them in the reference room or her house. No way could I have checked every book in the library."

"Why now, Mrs. Davis? Why after all these years, though?" Mark asked.

Mrs. Davis shrugged. "The same as Buck, I imagine. He came back because of his daughter and her fiancé's son. I didn't know why he was back, but I knew I had to find that information before he did. So I called my old friend, Bill, who'd come to me the first time with his idea of blackmailing Burke. I, of course, only wanted to save my library."

Mark nodded. He did know that, but there's one thing he didn't know. "I have to ask, Mrs. Davis. How did you connect Edda's death with the Burkes?"

She smiled, even sitting in a jumpsuit in county lock up, she was the same old Mrs. Davis he'd known since he was a child. "Jessica found the first piece.

The Library

She'd been riffling through some old boxes in the back when she found some photographs from a benefit held at the library in the thirties. She'd been so excited because the man in the picture looked so much like her fiancé. And he did. When she showed me a picture of Gregory, and I realized he was one of the Burkes, I got angry. I hadn't realized she'd been dating the man who wanted to shut down the library." Mrs. Davis leaned back. "Ironic, huh? The man who'd wanted to shut down my library was related to one of the benefactors who'd tried to save it."

Mark nodded, but let her continue.

"So I started looking through the microfilm for the benefit. I thought, what if I could find all the names of the people who'd attended years earlier? Maybe they'd be willing to help again if they were still alive or if, like Burke, their families were wealthy. But what I found in the microfilm only a few days after the library benefit was the tragic murder of the woman in the picture. Though shredded and discolored, it was clear that she was wearing the same dress. Somehow, someone had made sure that the picture Jessica had found was never in the papers."

Mark shook his head at the unbelievable coincidence. Three men in the Burke family had dated

Ashlyn's relatives. Two had tried to murder the women they'd once loved, and one had succeeded. "So, where's the picture?"

Mrs. Davis tilted her head. "It wasn't with the other items? That was the biggest piece of evidence. That photo put Wesley Burke Sr. with Edda days before the police found her murdered, and she was even in the same dress. He had to have killed her that very night."

"No," Mark said. "Not that we need it, though. Everyone responsible for all those unnecessary deaths is dead."

***

Laura Allan gazed at the picture of her grandmother and the man who looked so much like Gregory, the only man she'd ever loved, one final time before she burned it.

It's never the end, as there's always one more story to share.
Please read on to assist me with the next story in the series.

Before you go...

Dear friend, I hope you enjoyed *The Library*. Detective Mark Waters made his debut as a supporting character in the short story *The Pit Stop (This Stop Could be Life or Death)*. So if you enjoyed *The Depot* and *The Library*, please check it out as well.

I'd like to give a shoutout to Kim Stapf. Not only has Kim read every one of my books, she won the name-the-place-of-my-next-book contest. It is because of Kim that *The Library* took place in, well, the library. It was a wonderful recommendation on her part. I hope I did your suggestion justice, Kim.

Initially, I'd planned to write a series of one-hour reads, but since my lovely readers insisted I write a full novel with Detective Waters, and insisted he and

Before you go...

Ashlyn got their happily ever after, I think I will have to end his story, but I've been known to change my mind. Mark and Ashlyn could open a detective agency, investigating unsolved murders or paranormal events. Heck, we could even start on their honeymoon ... at some historical hotel.

I think I'm leaning toward Anna, though, our lovely redheaded forensic scientist. I've never written a novel with a female lead as an officer or similar position, as it requires more research than I already do for my stories. I also thought about cleaning up Detective Tim Townsend, see how he fares as a main character. Of course, there's always Captain Davis. At fifty-one, he's still young enough that he could move on to another career. And then ... if you've already read *The Pit Stop* with Detective Gino Canale, I contemplated continuing his story.

The point of me telling you this is that I love reader feedback. Several of my novels are a direct result of requests from readers — like this book. So if there's something you'd like to see in this series, please leave your notes in the review or connect with me via one of my cyber residences. You can always find me chatting

Before you go...

away on Twitter, Facebook, and Instagram, and I always respond to comments on my website.

Although all of my stories have a common thread — romance, mystery, and suspense — not all of my novels are supernatural. My first five books are romantic-suspense whodunits. They are all stand-alone novels; however, I do link each of my stories with a little surprise. I also write paranormal romantic suspense, the Creatus series. You can find links to all my books on my website, www.CarmenDeSousaBooks.com.

Please ... please ... please ... if you enjoyed this story, leave a review. It doesn't have to be fancy, just a few words to let other readers know if they should download it too. It means so much to an author to hear what readers loved — even didn't love — about a book. It's how we grow and learn what you want to read next time ... and in the case of a series, which characters you want to see more of in the next books or which ones we should knock off.

Thank you again!

Carmen